Eye of the Storm

To Jenn –

Hope you like my 1st book!

Eye of the Storm

sequel coming 2016

Aimee Kuzenski

By Aimee Kuzenski

BOOKMEN
Media Group
Minneapolis

Bookmen Media Group, Inc
331 Main Street South
Rice Lake, WI 54868
www.bookmenmediagroup.com

Ordering Information:
Quantity sales. Special discounts are available on quantity purchases by corporations, associations, and others. For details, contact the publisher at the address above.

ISBN 978-0-9884071-0-7

First Edition

2013943183

Printed in the United States of America
18 17 16 15 14 13 / 6 5 4 3 2 1

To Mom and Dad.

I hope you like your new grandchild.

1

Taking the Bait

"Ziggy, dammit! Stop it!"

The dog growled, spitting foam on wet pavement and straining at the end of its leash. I regarded the wiry-haired mutt with distaste and didn't bother glancing up at the young man restraining his dog. He yanked one last time, and the animal fell backward and scurried behind its owner. The barking diminished to grumbling snarls, hurled at me between his legs.

The man's wiry shoulders hunched as he gave me an embarrassed grin. I repressed a sigh; submission without a good fight is no victory at all. I raised a disapproving eyebrow at the young man and then smiled down at his angry little cur. At sight of my expression, the dog broke off its growl with a yelp and began to whine, now curling into a frightened ball. My smile widened.

"Geez mister, I'm sorry," stammered the dog's owner. Taken up with trying to control the animal, he'd probably missed my expression. Lucky for him. "She usually doesn't bark at all, much less go off on people like this." I glanced up at his face and noted with no surprise that he wouldn't look me in the eye. His gaze was fixed on my long, military-issue duster and nondescript button-down shirt and slacks. Even though my clothes had never been as interesting as my face, they'd always been easier for most people to look at.

I cocked my head at him, momentarily diverted from the morning's errand. The smile still tugged at the corners of my mouth, tinged now with disbelief. "Ziggy?" I queried. An odd name.

The man relaxed at my words. My voice is my best feature—mellifluous and chocolatey, not many have strength to resist its charm. Behind him, Ziggy the dog lowered her whine to a whisper.

"Yeah," he said, warming to his subject. "my wife is a big fan of that show, Quantum Leap. Ziggy was the computer's name."

This era and its preoccupation with television.

I dismissed his inane banter and glanced across the busy Manhattan street. Once my attention turned, Ziggy renewed her attack. She raced back around to lunge at me again, showing the whites of her eyes above gnashing yellow teeth. The young man cursed under his breath as he pulled the leash even tighter.

"She's usually so friendly. I don't know what's wrong with her." He was having trouble holding back the dog, despite her small size.

I chuckled, and Ziggy cut off mid-bark, her claws skittering against the sidewalk as she scraped to a halt. The young man's blue eyes widened.

"Dogs don't tend to like me," I said pleasantly.

"A cat person, are you?" His voice wavered on the last word, knuckles white on the leash.

Shrugging, I replied, "Cats don't like me, either."

Ziggy's owner stared at me fixedly. A muscle quivered beneath one eye. My lips stretched into a broad grin, and I leaned close to touch my right forefinger to his Adam's apple. His skin twitched beneath my finger, but he didn't move. He couldn't.

"I suggest you take your questions elsewhere, young man," I told him. "You're far too nosy for your own good."

I withdrew my fingertip slowly and let the spell break. The man staggered back, gagging, then spun and took to his heels, dragging his dog yapping close behind.

Pulling on my customary mask of civility, I adjusted my fedora and continued on my way. The skies were growing darker. I smelled another spring storm in the air.

I strolled through the thick lunchtime crowd, nodding and tipping my hat to ladies whose gazes crossed mine. The women I acknowledged smiled and blushed, casting their eyes down in a becoming expression of femininity.

I tried not to smile back at them. It would ruin the effect. People like to think that they are modern and civilized, that they don't believe in the monster under the bed or the evil witch in the woods. Their hindbrains know better when confronted with my smile. So do their pets.

I reached my destination with the spring from the short confrontation still in my step. My lawyer's office stood in a fashionable and expensive part of town, where the suit and briefcase quotient was high. The old, two-story brownstone was weathered and oozed history and the respectability of age. I breathed it in, slitting my eyes in pleasure. It reminded me of home, despite my home's relative youth.

What can I say? I'm a traditionalist. Old things please me.

I removed my hat as I walked through the heavy glass doors. The clerk at the oaken front desk nodded respectfully to me as he marked his place in a Latin text of the Aeneid with a tattered red ribbon.

His voice sounded younger than he looked. "Good afternoon, Mr. Sekhmet." I repressed my habitual smile at the name, not in the mood to deal with another scene. Sekhmet had been the Egyptian deity of violence and war. I am a traditionalist, and I also have a sense of humor. "Your weekly appointment with Mr. Dorsey, sir?" His thin, ink-stained fingers thumbed through the large appointment book to find today's date. The boy was actually George Dorsey's son, Ian, but I appreciated his ritual avoidance of that fact. Proper manners were part of what I paid for.

I nodded acknowledgment and shrugged out of my coat as he fluttered around to take it. He was a slight, scholarly young man and always seemed surprised by the weight of the long wool duster. Careful not to touch me as he took possession, he hung the hat and coat in the hall closet. I ran my thumbs under my suspenders to lay them flat against my chest and then settled in one of the brown overstuffed leather chairs to wait, crossing one ankle over the opposite knee.

The clerk returned to the front desk and lifted the melamine handset of his ancient rotary phone. He brought it to his ear and spun the dial once.

"Mr. Dorsey? Mr. Sekhmet is here to see you." He paused, listening. "Yes, sir. He replaced the handset with a soft, discreet click.

"Mr. Dorsey is ready to see you, Mr. Sekhmet. May I escort you to his office?" His outstretched hand trembled.

Faced with young Mr. Dorsey's nervous features, I felt a sharp bite of impatience. I declined with an irritated, flat-handed gesture. "Thank you, but no. I know the way."

He let out a tiny puff of pent-up breath and responded with an automatic, "Yes, sir." Clearly, he preferred to be left in the lobby without me.

I pushed myself out of the chair and walked over to the curving staircase, my steps muffled by thick red carpet. I reached the landing halfway up the flight and glanced back to see the young man abruptly look down, bending his crane-like features over his book.

I considered the boy's rudeness and decided to have a word with Dorsey about it. I did not pay premium fees to be ogled.

I resumed my course down the dark paneled hall. My lawyer's office door was ajar, letting out a spill of electric light. I preferred gas or oil lighting, and Dorsey knew it. Burying a worm of annoyance with an effort, I pushed the door open.

Dorsey's office was a large wainscoted room, and Dorsey himself sat at the far end behind his wide Victorian desk. The man couldn't be more unlike his son. He was as round as his son was thin, sporting his usual sober suit with a red silk tie knotted at his throat. His skin was unusually pale, an oily sheen of sweat was on his bald pate, and his left hand twitched where it lay next to a silver letter opener shaped like a dagger.

When his right hand dropped below the surface of his desk, a thrill of surprise ran through me and I settled my weight on the balls of my feet, coiled and ready to move in any direction. My hand still on the crystal doorknob, I waited for his first thrust. Through the prickle of excitement at the prospect of battle, I felt an unexpected twinge. I'd liked Dorsey.

Pushing the unwanted emotion aside, I kept my gaze fixed on the center of Dorsey's chest. Not much could get through my defenses, but I would be foolish to assume that would always be true. Jaw clenched, I waited.

When he brought a wooden crucifix up out of his lap, however, I couldn't help myself. I burst out laughing.

Dorsey flinched violently; more than one person had compared my laughter to anguished screams. To his credit, he didn't curl into a fetal ball or throw himself beneath his desk. He merely looked away, and the crucifix in his fist didn't waver.

"I know what you are," he blustered.

I restrained myself, grinning at him. "Oh, I very much doubt it." I turned my back on him and the room to close the door. I sensed his fear rising. When I turned back, he stood to wrap both hands around the base of the crucifix. He held it shakingly at arm's length.

I walked casually to the edge of his desk and leaned on its polished surface. Dorsey stumbled back with a squeak and fell back into his chair. The crucifix clattered against his desk and landed soundlessly on the carpeted floor.

"Get away from me!" he panted, stark white and panic-stricken. I winced at the noise. The sounds of terror had never pleased me. Impatient, I closed one fist tight, and his voice went silent, his eyes bugging.

"Dorsey," I chided, "you are both right and wrong. Right, in deducing that I am not now, nor have I ever been, human."

He shuddered, his retreat attempting to burrow backward through his chair. Dorsey's high forehead was beaded with sweat. I felt my upper lip curl in a snarl.

"Wrong," I continued, "in believing that your tired, overused symbol could stop me." Dorsey gasped shallow breaths as though my breath stank. It probably did. I was fast moving from amused to annoyed, and fires roared to life in my chest, belching sulfur fumes.

Leaning even further across the desk, I stated, "I am no demon subject to your God, nor a fallen angel ruling the depths of hell, nor a ghost, nor a fairy lord." The nerve, nay, the gall of these pathetic creatures, swiping at what they couldn't possibly understand, disrupting my routine.

Dorsey's eyes narrowed, and I studied him through a red haze. Under his roiling fear, was he curious?

I watched his thoughts flail as he tried to anticipate my words. My sneer dropping away, I stated, "I am War incarnate, Dorsey. That cross has been on my banners for years at a time. You cannot threaten me with it."

His jaw dropped, and he took a deep, utterly silent breath. One hand clenched and scrabbled for the letter opener atop the desk.

I reached out to take Dorsey by one lapel and dragged him upright. He brought up his blunt, soft-metaled weapon in an unschooled thrust; I blocked it with barely a thought and flicked the blade from his palm with one thumb to the hilt. Shaking my head, I growled, "I like you, Dorsey, despite this betrayal. You even seem to be a warrior somewhere inside that civilized mask. But I am War, and I cannot leave you alive, not when I cannot trust you, nor can I give you a gentle death."

He squirmed silently, his hands clamped around my right wrist. His lips formed a flurry of words, his face flooding with urgency. A breath away from Dorsey's execution, I paused. Curiosity warred with my temper and won. I gave him back his voice.

Hands locked around my fist at his lapel, Dorsey burst out, "You can't kill me! You need me!" His chest heaved as though I'd been denying him air as well as his voice.

My fist tightened. "I need you," I repeated, tasting the unlikely words. Seeming to miss my building fury, Dorsey bobbed his head, his persona clicking into the satisfied manipulator I'd seen so often in this very office.

He bared his teeth at me, less of a grin than a dare. "She warned me about you, Sekhmet. If you kill me, you'll lose everything I've helped you build. I've destroyed everything." The man stank of fear, his hands clammy on mine. "All of your business is in my head! You'll never recover one file or contact if you get rid of me!"

I felt one finger, then two rip through the thick wool of Dorsey's jacket. The lawyer flinched.

I smiled at him. "I have recovered from worse."

I reached back with my left hand to draw the sword of my office from its invisible sheath and watched Dorsey's face go slack and pale. Lifting the little worm fully off the floor, I whirled the short, infantry-style gladius and swept it forward in a smooth, graceful arc to part Dorsey's head from his shoulders. The razor-sharp blade whispered contentment as it sliced between vertebrae without a hitch. It was bloody, rank, and intoxicating. I hadn't killed by my own hand in decades.

When my heart rate eased, I sheathed my sword. Letting Dorsey's headless body fall away from me, I felt my jaw muscles clench and my teeth creak.

He had said, "She warned me."

I scrubbed at my face with one hand, abruptly at a loss. As good as that rage had felt, it may have led me into an immense tactical error. Somehow, someone had warned Dorsey about me, albeit with incomplete information. And with wild abandon, I had just destroyed my only path to that enemy. Not for the first time, I cursed my berserker's nature. My hands itched for something else to reduce to splinters.

I gazed down at the body of my lawyer. It would be a dishonor to both of us to leave him this way, never mind how it would compound the danger of my situation. Shaking my head, I felt a familiar surge of frustration. My strengths were in the heat of battle, not its aftermath. Now, with my red haze cleared, I surveyed the wreckage, empty of ideas.

Dorsey lay crumpled beside his chair, headless and still. The head itself lay tipped to one side on the broad glossy desk, expressionless now and surrounded by a slowly growing halo of gore. Blood dripped soundlessly to the rugs, blending the red and gold both into dark crimson. Soon it would dry to a displeasing brown, but for the moment at least, it was beautiful.

Shaking the fancy from my thoughts, I examined the entire room, the pristine woodwork and restored ceiling worth thousands and thousands of dollars, priceless in historical value. With a sigh, I pulled a spark from inside me to manifest in the palm of my hand, bobbing firefly-like. I stared at it for a moment, then shrugged and tossed it to the dry, hundred-year-old rug at my feet.

The spark took root immediately, growing and multiplying into a supernaturally hot and hungry fire. As it spread, wood charred and darkened, fibers flared like tinder, tin warped and sagged. I witnessed its swift passing, though it gave me no pleasure. Would that I were still on good terms with my siblings! My sister could have cleansed this place of gore and its inhabitants of memories with a simple exertion of her considerable will, but I had not worked with her in nearly three millennia. This would not be the first time the fallout of that quarrel had cost me.

Dorsey's body was on fire in seconds as though it were dry kindling, the stench of burning flesh mixing with woodsmoke and the tang of hot metal. I opened the door and the flames followed me in a ruddy wave. The lobby wavered in and out of view. When I got past the smoke, the great front desk was empty. Young Ian must have left at the first hint of fire. Cowardly, but it fit his trembling façade.

I lingered as I took the stairs, caressing the silken banister for the last time. Smoke had already flowed to the lobby, and the front doubled doors were wide open. Sirens blared in the distance. The neighborhood warranted a quick response, it appeared. I took my coat and fedora from the hall closet and walked through the smoke and flames to the rear exit. This door was locked and barred. Willing it open with a thought, I strode out into the empty alley, leaving behind the angry crackling of the blaze. A few hundred yards from the building, I turned back.

The brownstone was a complete loss, already shooting gouts of flame and black smoke from every window. As I watched, the roof fell in with a deafening crash.

Mortals have said that War had no mercy, no pity, no understanding of loss. This was not true—I do have those feelings.

They simply did not rule my actions.

The gym stank of old rubber, plastic, leather, and the sweat soaked and ground into every inch. None of the regulars responded when opening the door to greet the characteristic ambiance. It smelled like home.

Olivia Fatunbi worked a heavy bag in the corner, her gray tank top darkened to charcoal with perspiration. Her partner grunted with each impact.

"Jesus, woman. Let me throw at least a few punches before we go on-shift." Rob Quinn's tape-wrapped fingers tightened to absorb his partner's next punch, which, as expected, was harder than the norm. Sweat dripped from his close-cropped scalp.

"Shut up, asshole," Olivia grunted. "You had the first half hour, I get the second. That's how it works." Her dark skin gleamed.

"Yeah, yeah." He gave her bent head a crooked smile and backed away from the bag, hands up. "But that half hour ended ten minutes ago."

Olivia threw a mock-serious punch that he ducked. Chortling, Quinn took off for the men's locker room.

"You getting any this weekend?" He yelled over his shoulder. Olivia smothered a laugh. Good God, the man had no filter.

Rolling her eyes hugely, Olivia grinned back. "That's not how it is with Camilla, and you know it!" She began unwrapping her hands, angling toward her own shower.

Quinn hooted, and the owner grinned from his dark corner. "Right. And I'm chief of police." Stepping around a pair of men wrestling on the mats, he added, "You two are like two peas in a pod, except you're a detective, and she's a lieutenant." One of the wrestlers snorted and was summarily thrown into a smooth arm lock. Quinn pointed and laughed, momentarily diverted.

Olivia closed her eyes for a fraction of a second to revel in the still unfamiliar freedom of being out as a lesbian both at work and the gym. It had only been a few months. "Army lieutenant outranks any cop," Olivia yelled back, "and a boxing workout isn't exactly a date, either." She ducked into the locker room to end the conversation. On the way to the showers, she checked her phone.

"Shit," she muttered, then leaned over to pound the wall adjoining the men's locker room with her fist.

"Make it quick! There's a fire uptown and it looks like it's our case for the day."

Ian Dorsey sat with his head in his singed hands, across the street from his father's ruined office. The air stank of wet ash and the chemicals used to put out the fire.

Only a few hours ago, he'd been safely ensconced behind the lobby desk of his father's office, greeting clients and researching lesson plans for Greek in Translation or Latin II as he had been for the whole of this summer.

Now, he sat shell-shocked on the curb, his cell phone gone, the book he'd been reading burnt to cinders, and his father's body charred into an unrecognizable carbon rock somewhere in the destroyed building in front of him.

He stared numbly at the trash in the gutter between his knees, unable to think beyond the last moment he'd spent in that building.

Waist-deep in the Aeneid, he had assumed the unsettling Mr. Sekhmet would take his usual two hours out of the afternoon. The building had been quiet, beyond the creaks and sighs common to something that old. He'd gotten through a few dozen pages of Virgil. Then, after less than half an hour, a great whumpf had sounded upstairs and the front double doors blew open. Ian had jerked out of the precision of Latin language structure to see waves of flame shooting out his father's office door. Leaping to his feet, he'd sprung around the desk like a startled cat, on the verge of hurtling himself up the stairs to rescue Dad.

That's when Ian had seen him, when the whole world had gone sideways.

Mr. Sekhmet had emerged from the inferno without so much as a spark kindled on his hair or clothing, accompanied by thick, acrid smoke. The snapping, biting fire ate around and under Sekhmet's feet, framing him like a curling aura. Responding to animal instinct, Ian had slammed on the brakes and ducked under the stairwell where he couldn't be seen.

Like a fucking rabbit, Ian. With your father burning to death upstairs!

Ian shook his head, hands balling into tighter fists. Those internal voices were getting louder.

Again, Ian shook his head violently, this time until his ears rang. It simply wasn't possible, but he knew what he'd seen. His father's strangest, most profitable client had walked out of a blazing fire, taken the time to pick up his coat and hat, and left through a sealed door with a mere touch of his hand.

God in heaven, what is going on? Closing his eyes, Ian dug one knuckle into his temple, his vision going blurry with the pressure. Gentle fingers closed on Ian's shoulder, and his heart stuttered. He jerked away in shock and slapped those hands away, hard.

You're such a beast, Ian! No wonder you're all alone, you deserve it!

Ian twitched, a tic he was coming to suspect would be with him for a long time. Oh God, his medication had been in the office, too. His pulse hammered in his chest and shaking fingers. It ramped up a notch when he saw the white uniform, the flashing lights whirling behind it.

The EMT who had touched him stepped back, her own hands raised. Her face was taut, as though she were afraid of him.

And so she should be!

"Shut up, shut up!" he hissed aloud. The EMT, small and pale, backed away a little further.

"Mr. Dorsey?" Her voice was smooth, with a violin string of tension humming through it. "Ian Dorsey? Your father's landlord identified you. Are you hurt?" she asked carefully. She looked above Ian's head and motioned someone closer. "The police want to talk to you, too, about the fire." Ian wrenched around to see a large man in office clothes with a bright badge hanging from his breast pocket approaching, right hand on his gun. Catching himself on the curb, Ian could feel the grainy surface of concrete under his fingers scraping them raw.

They're here to take you in, Ian! They're blaming you!

"I'm fine, I'm fine!" Ian sputtered frantically. Not a jail cell, dear God no! He scrambled to get his feet under him, to crab-walk away from his fate collapsing in. The voices in his head went on and on and on …

He struggled when they laid hands on him, but he knew it was pointless. His fist connected with flesh, and the cop grunted. Cursing, he immediately twisted Ian's hands behind him and half-carried him to the antiseptic embrace of the waiting ambulance.

Ian kicked and yelled. Broken phrases poured from his lips, and he began to sob in deep gasping breaths. Blurrily, Ian could see the cop assisting the EMT in strapping both of his wrists to the surface of a gurney. As the ambulance doors closed, Ian had one coherent thought in the windstorm of his mind: Sekhmet had killed his father, and that bastard would pay for it, even if it was Ian's final act.

"Wow." Olivia watched the bus wail its way off to the hospital, scratching at the short-cropped curls under her cap.

Quinn shook his head. "No shit. I wonder what he's on."

She grimaced. "Could be any number of things. Might not even be drugs, might be hard-wired." Turning to look at the smoldering brownstone, Olivia inhaled sharply and coughed at the smoke in the air.

Quinn let her have a moment. Fires were hard for Olivia, and he knew it. It was less than six months since her mother had died.

"At least it looks cut and dried." Rob always knew when to cut back and be professional—damn good partner.

Olivia kept her gaze on the charred hulk across the street. "We're nailing that son of a bitch to the wall."

"If he did it." Dammit, did he think she didn't know that?

Olivia's movements were getting sharp and angry, kicking stones into the road. "I am not losing a firebug, Quinn."

He sighed. "I know a doc at the ER, owes me a favor. I'll make sure he gets to the interrogation room."

That was more like it. She stopped trying to kick gravel across the street. "Good." Spine stick straight, Olivia looked back over her shoulder. Go on, say it. "And you should probably be the one to talk to him."

Quinn nodded, not even bothering to keep the relief from his face, then turned back to the car. Olivia leashed her temper and followed.

2

Family Problems

I returned to my home, rid of one problem only to have gained a large set of new ones.

The Alexander Sekhmet identity would be a liability from now on. Ian Dorsey seemed likely to have escaped the fire, and either he assumed me dead, suspected me as an arsonist and murderer, or (potentially the worst option) he saw me leaving a burning building through a locked door.

I hardly expected the police to believe that, but others might. I have never been without enemies. I tested the wards around my lands again, considered strengthening them. No, that was paranoia speaking.

I sat down to consider my options, a glass of single malt chilling my fingers. I knocked it back and felt the cold scotch burn all the way down, then set the empty crystal glass down on a nearby coaster.

If today had not happened—if events had proceeded as they had my entire modern existence—I would have been prepared, having laid down financial bolt-holes and paper trails for my next identity. My company would now pass smoothly into "new" hands, with my suppliers and customers unaware of anything unusual. It would appear that the old identity had died of natural causes and had in his will passed on his business to a son, brother, nephew, whomever.

And while I'd begun this process already, all of the work had been with Dorsey. As he had sneered before I'd silenced him permanently. That was a critical lapse in judgment on my part, and not the first of my long life. I had once been so calm, so focused, immune to insult and flattery alike. Now … well. That decision was immutable and far in the past.

I tapped the crystal next to me, listened to the chime. I could start over completely, set myself up as an upstart grabbing business from my suddenly headless company. That scenario had served me well before. That had also, however, been a few centuries ago, when records were not so well tracked and travel was not so restricted.

I heaved a sigh. War was not subtle. I could have silenced Dorsey no other way. It was not in my nature. My siblings would have dealt with him much differently, though it seemed likely they would not have needed to deal with him at all. Of the four of us, my personality was the hardest to conceal.

Would that I could wield my siblings' powers! Conquest would have spun Dorsey's head with words until he trusted her more than his son sitting downstairs. Plague would have cheerfully infested him with something deadly until he broke. And Death—the head of our Family—would have needed no more than a smile and a crook of his bony finger.

As though on cue, a light breath touched my mind, and I stiffened. A Family member had crossed the border of my land. Quashing a tendril of surprised irritation, I snared the mind of a crow perched on my roof. Its black cabochon eyes showed me a small, neat figure waiting a decorous distance from my home. Alarm abated, curiosity rose. The Messenger.

I had seen very few of my Family in the past centuries. My left eye twitching, I wondered if the anonymous "she" had sent Hermes to crow over today's events.

Of course, that would make today's mess a Family matter, and I doubted any of us was foolish enough to risk the consequences.

The doors opened as I approached, framing my brother-cousin in steel that matched his dove gray suit. His mercurial eyes were a bright red. I acknowledged his display of my color and returned that courtesy with a shallow dip of my chin.

"Messenger." I opened my arms, offering him entrance. "Be welcome in my house."

He wore the same human-like aspect he'd had when last we'd met. Slight, well-muscled, and costumed so blandly that the eye slid past him. A thin smile curled his lips. He crossed my threshold, eyes blinking back to their usual silver. "War," he said, his voice as smooth as ever. "I accept your welcome."

Traditional greetings past, I ushered Hermes into my study. I did not offer him my scotch. He seated himself, unbuttoning his jacket and straightening the crease of his trousers. I sat in my high-backed office chair and kept the granite and steel desk between us.

Hermes' smile thinned to a knife-edge. "Very well, Ares. To business." I could feel the tallying of points in his mind, calculating what of this conversation he could sell to other Family members.

I waited and anticipated another glass of cold scotch.

His eyes were locked on mine. My brother-cousin, Messenger and spy. "I bring a message from Apollo."

I did my best to keep my reaction from my face. The Oracle? I'd last seen him a couple centuries ago, opium pipe in hand. I had no time for fever dreams today. Teeth clenching, I motioned him to continue.

"You are in danger, brother-cousin." His voice was over-serious, as though he spoke to a wayward child.

Well. Perhaps this was a true seeing, though I would have preferred to receive warning before the scene with Dorsey. I sighed. "His warning is late, as usual."

Hermes tilted his rounded chin upward, showing me a gray collar, gray silk tie, gray, gray, gray. I brushed my hand through my black hair. My fingers begged to tighten around his elegant neck, to expend my frustration with violence and clear my mind. The Messenger was no one's friend.

"As you wish. Better to be cautious, yes?" He shifted and rose to his feet. "Apollo insisted I speak with you now, however, and as he was wreathed in less poppy smoke than is his wont, I suggest you heed him. He said your day still had hours on the clock." What did he dangle in front of me with this? Games like this were why I had left the Family behind.

I shut my eyes briefly, fighting the snarl behind my lips. "Very well, brother-cousin. I thank you." I fished a gold coin from my pocket and stood to offer it. He nipped it from my hand, quick as a swallow. Itching to return to my thoughts, I showed him to the door.

He stopped at the threshold to look squarely at me, eyes shifting color in a rainbow blur. "Ares. Please tell me the story behind this visit, soon." He patted his breast pocket where the gold coin laid. "Information is good currency."

Why wouldn't he simply leave? "I have already paid you, Messenger."

His teeth flashed in a gentle grin. "Perhaps I should ask your sister. Conquest is the general, after all, not you. War alone is nothing but strife."

I threw the doors open with an angry thought. "Out!"

Hermes settled the cuffs of his shirt, opal cuff links flickering, and beat an unruffled retreat. I made sure he left my property, snagging the mind of a nearby crow to watch him go. He had always reveled in pricking my temper, once I acquired it.

I stared at the closed doors, fists clenching on empty air. What did this mean? This had to be internal. If other Families were moving on ours, there would be no time for childish games. Or was Apollo just the excuse for my Family to bait me? Their politics were ridiculous, verging on insane. The risks they took to alleviate boredom could not be reconciled with reality.

I would not let Hermes' visit distract me this way. Wincing, I reined in my mind to the task at hand: How would I move forward after this morning's debacle? Starting fresh did not appeal to me; even leaving aside the difficulties inherent in today's culture, I simply had no enthusiasm for a tactic so worn and fraught with uncertainties.

I shook myself and paced back to the marble floor of my sitting room, the heels of my Italian shoes click-clacking in time with my frustration.

These worn-out strategies felt all wrong. The times had changed, and I had not changed with them. My greatcoat, my fedora, my preference for outdated customs and architecture were all symbols of what was holding me back. Perhaps I should move in an entirely new direction. I must do more than merely survive. I needed to thrive. If I failed, war would spread unfettered across the earth. It would be complete anarchy, exactly what I'd had to rein in when my brother gave me this dominion millennia ago. I shivered in disgust, then chuckled at my reaction. If that were to happen, at least I would not live to see it. Knowing the uproar that would cause in the Family would almost be worth the loss, though.

Stopping before my large bay window that overlooked the military academy of West Point, I drank in the comforting sharp lines. Gray-clad cadets marched smoothly in formation, square-shaped groups snapping turns in time to the barked and peppery commands of their sergeants. One group stood at attention while their lieutenant presented an award for valor. Her blond hair was in a tight bun under her cap.

I went still. For the great bulk of my existence, women had been involved in war mainly as victims or prizes, rarely as generals or warriors. Only recently had that changed.

Staring down at the woman with lieutenant's bars on her shoulder, a plan bloomed in my head like a bloody red rose.

"General? The dean can see you right away, sir."

The three glittering stars on my shoulder had taken me past the dean's guard dog with charming alacrity. I nodded genially to the young man and walked into the office of the head of West Point. It glowed with sunlight, reflected off the caramel walls and the copper squares of plaques. The slight, silver-haired dean was hunched over an open file and glanced up as I entered. His blue eyes winced at me, and he levered himself to his feet.

"General. How may I help you?" His light voice was frayed and ragged at the edges. He brushed imaginary dust from the two stars at his shoulder.

I seated myself in the armchair in front of his desk and nodded him into his own, smiling to myself when he winced again. Quashing the expression as well as I could, I went into my act. I sighed, running one hand over my freshly sheared crew cut.

"General Wilson. I have a favor to ask of you." Letting myself sag back into the upholstery, I squinted up at him. "I might even be able to take some trouble off your hands as well."

He folded gnarled hands and lifted one eyebrow. "Oh really?" A wry grin creased his face. "You're talking my language now, sir."

I brushed off the honorific with a manufactured scowl. "Please don't 'sir' me, Dean. This is your office, after all, and I need a favor."

The tension bled a bit from his shoulders, and his expression smoothed. "Fine, General . . . ?"

"Hayes." I hoped the army general in front of me would not catch the reference to Admiral Hayes of the US Navy. My preference for names that meant something seemed childish now. My impulsiveness led me down dangerous roads, for the second time in one day. The chair I sat in was abruptly uncomfortable.

The dean didn't bat an eye. "General Hayes. Down to brass tacks, then. What can I do for you today?"

My gaze moved over his desk, taking in family photos, a worn cigar box, nicotine stains on the tips of his fingers. I let a snarl float across my face as I took in his masculine surroundings and felt his interest sharpen.

Rolling my shoulders backward as if to release tension, I let one hand curl into a fist. In his sight, of course.

"It has been brought to my attention that my office lacks gender diversity." I shook myself as though bugs crawled along my spine and showed the general a weary smile. No teeth, though. "I'm hoping you can help me find a lieutenant I could use to show my superiors why I prefer to keep women out of my work."

Wilson paused, eyes widening a fraction, then broke forth in a loud guffaw. "All due respect, sir, but that's an odd request."

Interesting. Could the dismissive attitude I wore be less common than I expected? "I know it's frowned on these days, but it's still true that war is a man's job. I can't have a woman twisting my office into knots. She would be a distraction to the men and would demand more attention than she deserves." I caught his eyes registering reluctant approval and breathed a little easier.

He looked out the window to watch his cadets walking below. "General, I like your honesty, but I can't really think of anyone in my current pool of cadets who would be able to help you." He started to lean back, folding his hands, then stopped again. His eyes went thoughtful. "Though I do have one instructor I might be able to loan you." He pulled a thick file from a squat cabinet at his feet and offered it across his desk.

I took the file and opened it to the first page. After a moment of scanning, I couldn't restrain a chuckle.

"Perfect."

3

Camilla Is Snared

The mass of half-grown men in front of her dissolved into chaos, and First Lieutenant Camilla Sykes turned away. From long, hard-won habit, she kept her spine ramrod straight and marched off toward her own quarters as though on parade duty.

As essentially, she was. One misstep, and she'd be out of the army with nowhere to go.

Camilla Sykes had wanted to be a soldier for as long as she could remember. She'd taken karate and aikido classes from a very early age and had learned barrel-racing on her cousin's half-broken quarter horse. Gym had been her favorite subject in school, and she'd forced her way into the captain position of her high school rugby team. (She understood that the school board had responded by banning any further women from joining at all, after she'd graduated.)

And once she had graduated, there had been only one place she wanted to go: the nearest army recruiting station. She'd pushed herself to near collapse in basic training, flown through unarmed combat, and taken to guns like a teenage boy discovering porn. As a girl, she'd expected hazing and saw her share of it. Camilla had shrugged it all off. She'd passed out of basic at the top of her class.

Once she'd graduated to the real army, to a real combat zone, things changed. The hazing from her peers didn't stop. Her superiors got too close and suggested problems could be fixed "in private," and her angry, shocked reactions put her even further down the totem pole. She couldn't use the skills she'd sharpened at basic. She had to drive the Humvee or guard civilians. Camilla bit gracelessly at the bars they put around her for a year, marking time. Then finally, finally, the combat had come to her. Her troop-mates were trapped by enemy fire near Kirkuk. Radio broken by a stray bullet, she'd abandoned the Humvee to take her rifle on a circular track that gave her the jump on first one clump of enemy soldiers, then another. She'd met what was left of her troop dotted with blood and grime to help drag two wounded privates to the truck. She'd earned lieutenant's bars for that, a turn through officer training, and a post stateside when her tours were over.

Unsurprisingly, she hadn't taken well to home duty, either. After filing yet another pointless report for yet another sedentary almost-general, Camilla had finally let her temper loose. It had felt insanely good to tell the old man to shove his damn paperwork up his fat ass and give her something real to do. Unfortunately, her commanding officer hadn't been nearly as amused by it.

And so, she thought bitterly, I'm stuck at West Point, teaching cadets to respect the chain of command and handing out medals. And to these kids who will graduate as officers, I'll always be a grunt. I'll never be good enough.

She'd thought at first she could take it, that they couldn't make her quit. But after five years of this make-work, she wasn't nearly as certain.

"First Lieutenant Sykes."

Miss Sykes was deep in her thoughts and startled away from my greeting. I watched her step back so she didn't need to crane her neck to look me in the face, and I found myself repressing a wave of admiration.

Examining her quickly blank expression, I could see the tension in her neck, the muscles in her jaw working. She might have an iron grip on herself, but it cost her dearly. Strands of her dishwater blond hair had worked loose to fan over a tanned, pinched face with liquid dark eyes. Not a beauty by any standards, but she was clearly fit and healthy; that was far more important to me.

She glanced at my shoulder, and her eyes widened. No doubt, she thought a lieutenant general to be a bad sign.

"First Lieutenant Sykes?" I repeated. She gathered herself even tighter and nodded, a marionette's jerky bob.

"Yessir. May I be of assistance, sir?" Her tone bordered on hostile. I pulled back a grin. But was that even worth the effort?

I surveyed her, the control and the wariness in her eyes. Very well, then, another test. I bared my teeth in a lupine smile, not even blunting the edge of it. She paled, and her hands balled into petite fists, but she neither wavered nor stepped back. Excellent.

"Yes," I approved, "you are exactly who I need."

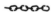

Sykes swallowed hard, and I saw blood on her lips. She'd bitten her tongue. "Sir." Despite her distress, she was still here, still fighting.

I turned sideways and ushered her solicitously forward on her previous course. "Lieutenant, my name is Hayes. I have an opportunity for you. May we speak privately?"

Her eyes narrowed, flicking from my insignia to my face. "Of course, sir. My office is just up the hill."

Not acceptable. "I'd rather more privacy than that. Are we near your quarters?"

She stared warily at me for a long moment, pressing her lips together. "Yes, sir. It's this way." Giving me a wide berth, she stepped around me and continued on her way. Moving like a wooden doll, she led me to her room.

The filthy police station was unbelievably loud: people shouting, talking on phones, slamming doors. Ian cringed at each painful noise, hunkering further into himself. He couldn't even get his hands over his ears effectively with both wrists cuffed together.

The hospital had reluctantly released him into the hands of the police very quickly after giving him a shot of haloperidol (which didn't do much of anything, unlike the last time he'd had a dose of that particular anti-psychotic) and determining he wasn't physically hurt. A series of handoffs from one doctor to another followed after his mental health record was retrieved. In the final exchange, Ian had seen money and a fat file folder pass between the doctor and the cop—the cop he'd seen at the fire—and he knew it had to be his medical history.

They'll find plenty to crow over in it, he thought with a twitch. Especially in the psych section. Dad had buried as much of his childhood run-ins with authority as possible, but it would only take a little digging to bring it all out—the early onset schizophrenia in high school, the vandalism, oh God, the fires, all of the meds that hadn't worked and the one that had. With a history like that, Ian knew the cops would never believe that he'd seen a supernatural being in his father's office, or that this being had probably started the fire. Ian wasn't sure if he believed it, himself.

When the voices took ascendancy like this, he couldn't believe much of what he saw or heard anymore.

You stupid fool! You left your father to die!

The problem was that this time, even with everything that had ever made sense telling him it couldn't be real, his memories of that person were hard to ignore. He realized his hands were shaking when the chain connecting them began to jingle softly.

The big beefy officer from the hospital fell into the chair next to him and Ian jumped, the cuffs rattling as he tried to jerk away. The cop cocked his head at him, smiling toothily. He raised his hands in apology.

"Hey Ian. Did I scare you? I'm sorry," liar "but you see, I'm just so wound up over that fire at your dad's office, I just can't think straight." The well-fed, unshaven face leaned in closer, pushing Ian back with garlic breath. "Now why don't you tell me just what happened out there, so we can all put our minds to rest, okay?"

Ian wanted to put up his arms again to protect himself from this intimidating man. He knew, though, that it was exactly the wrong thing to do. The bastard was just trying to scare him.

Too bad for Ian that it was working. He gulped and tried to sit up straighter.

Words burst out of him in a torrent. "Officer, I really—I don't know what happened! I was downstairs, in the lobby, reading a book."

That beautiful book, burnt to ashes! Your fault!

"And I—I'd just sent a client up to Dad about thirty minutes before. The next thing I knew, the f-fire was all over the stairs." Crap, was he going to have a stuttering fit? Ian clenched his fists tight, hoping the cop would listen to him.

Frowning, the cop leaned closer. Ian couldn't help but cringe back; the man was huge, and that fake goofy smile was gone.

"A client, you said? Someone else was up there with him?" Relief bloomed in his chest. Oh thank God, the cop was actually going to listen to him.

"Yes!" he rushed out, "Mr. Alexander Sekhmet was up there with him. But I was the only person on the first floor when I saw the fire."

Tell him about the man! Tell him what you saw; you have to!

"That's why you were the only one to get out?" The round face was getting even closer, eyes intense.

Tell him!

"Shut up, shut up, shut up!" Damn voices, why couldn't they just leave him alone?

The cop had gone still. Looking up, Ian realized that he'd spoken out loud. Shit. Shit!

You're such an idiot, Ian! Can't you keep your mouth shut?

Ian stuffed a fist over his mouth, his other hand hanging tense at his jaw, the wrists still tied together with handcuffs. He looked pleadingly up at the cop, who had backed off. His eyes were wide, and other people in the desk-crowded room were starting to turn to look.

Look at the freak. Look at the moron who left his father to die!

Unable to stay silent anymore, Ian burst out, "I didn't leave him to die, I didn't! I couldn't go up the stairs to save him, not with all that fire, and the man, the terrible man." He couldn't contain the words anymore. They were spurting out like water from a broken water main.

Abruptly, the cop knelt down in front of Ian, grabbing his shoulders and shaking him roughly. "What man, Ian? What man? Did your dad's client get out?" His face was intent, fierce. Ian grabbed fistfuls of the officer's shirt.

"Yes, yes he did! He just walked down the stairs, not on fire!"

You told him, Ian! Now you've done it!

He couldn't tell why the voices were angry now, but he couldn't stop the words from pouring out. "Then he took back his coat and hat and left through the back door. Why would he do that?" Ian was shaking, and he felt tears drip from his chin. The fluorescent lights above him bobbled and blinked.

The cop searched his face, then sighed and peeled himself away from Ian's grasp. He stood and looked back at someone in the room behind him.

"You'd better call in the doc," he said flatly. "I don't think I'm qualified to interrogate this subject."

From the back of the room, a voice volunteered, "Well, shit. And the shrink's in court today. I'll get a call out to his office; he might have a backup."

Ian sank back in his chair, clasped his hands, and began to rock, weeping in great sobbing gulps of air.

You idiot! You are a worthless waste of skin!

No, he thought weakly. No, I'm not.

"After you, sir."

Miss Sykes held the door into her quarters for me, turning my accustomed manners upside down. I withheld a grimace as I looked around. The small room was white, neat, and stark as a dry bone: the only scraps of personality were the four books stacked carefully on her nightstand and the silver liquor flask glittering from her otherwise empty desk. The novel at the top of the stack was a well-thumbed copy of The Left Hand of Darkness.

The small woman didn't appear to be pleased with her exile at West Point. I hoped it would make this task a bit less unpleasant.

I turned back to see the lieutenant cross her threshold, leaving the door wide open. I quashed the approval that her action brought to my lips. She understood the importance of leaving herself a way out. It showed good sense and an ability to keep her head under pressure.

Unfortunately for her, I didn't want anyone else seeing or overhearing us. I stepped behind her and closed the door.

I looked back to see her eyes narrowed, weighing me much as I'd weighed her earlier. If possible, her spine got even straighter as I turned to face her again. She nailed her gaze past my shoulder, avoiding my eyes.

"Sir," she ventured, "may I have permission to speak?" She was the picture of a good soldier, but I could feel her thoughts roiling around in her skull. Trying to keep my warming anticipation from my face, I nodded, watching her carefully.

The lieutenant gave the impression of agitated motion without moving an inch. Keeping her gaze on the door behind me, she asked, "Sir, I'm afraid I don't know you. Please, may I know why you're meeting with me in my own quarters? Are you investigating me, sir?" The last sentence rushed out as though she'd wanted it to be the first. In anticipation, Sykes held herself so tight she quivered.

I couldn't help but smile this time. It was good for Camilla that she was still focusing on her closed door. I took my cap from the crook of my arm and laid it next to the flask on her desk, watching her closely. She held herself still, but I saw the lieutenant's shoulders release a fraction as the path to her door cleared, then tense again as I passed behind her, out of view. Was that simple caution or battle fatigue?

"Lieutenant," I said, the smile coloring my voice, "I don't need to investigate you. I can take the measure of a soldier in one meeting." She shifted slightly as I walked a slow arc behind her. "I can see that you are the one who can accomplish what I need done."

Her frustration was starting to color the edges of her thoughts. She suddenly turned to face me, her expression hard. Interesting.

"With all due respect sir, I still don't know what that job is. A soldier goes where she is sent, but—I believe I deserve to know what I'll be doing." The delicate-seeming woman caught my eyes and stiffened. Lines of stress and worry returned to her face. "Sir."

Her career hadn't been kind to her. A pang of unexpected sympathy ached in my chest. I pulled out her plain wooden chair and arranged myself on it, pulling the creases on my trousers straight and sharp. Many find my height imposing, but I could usually put them more at ease by sitting. This young officer instead puffed up, her shoulders climbing another fraction of an inch, perhaps at the appropriation of her territory. I found myself wanting to chuckle at her angry kitten appearance. Small wonder she'd found herself trapped at West Point in a dead-end post with a temper like that.

I decided then to speak the truth to her, though the context would definitely be misleading. "I need perspective, lieutenant. I am one of the old guard, so to speak, and it's come to my attention that I haven't kept up with the times. You, Sykes, are exactly what I need to bring me into this century. And I need you now." I stared at her, obliquely wondering why I was arguing. I could just take her and be done with it, even though the process would work more smoothly if she agreed to it.

So, I settled further into her chair. "I've spoken to the dean, and he had no issue with your reassignment. Do not worry that you will be treated as a glorified secretary." I smiled again, teeth bared, and watched blood drain from her face. A blow well marked. She'd certainly registered the expression that time. "Your record speaks for itself on that subject. What did you call that brigadier general? 'A misogynistic fuckwad?'" Embarrassment painted Sykes bright red.

She looked down briefly to regain her poise, then locked eyes with me again. My respect for her raised a significant fraction. Very few will look at me directly after trying it once. Parry, and counterstrike, I thought. Had she been born male, she'd likely be well on her way to a grand military career by now. It was really a pity.

"Sir," she said, nodding sharply, "I'm all yours." She reached out her right hand. Stomach churning with unexpected tension, I stood to clasp it.

4

Setting Boundaries

When our palms met, a shock went through my arm into her hand and the lieutenant's eyes went wide.

I closed my eyes, and for the first time in millennia, I shed my material form and slid into Sykes' bloodstream like a hit of heroin. Her nerves sparked with commands that I silenced as I passed them. I took quick possession of one pathway after another as I made my way to her brain. Camilla flailed at me, the shock and confusion of my attack not enough to paralyze her, but I batted her away as she might have swatted at a fly and settled into the command center of her nervous system, testing filaments and reaction time. To my surprise, Sykes came in again for a more organized attack. She slammed into me with the mental equivalent of a haymaker, rebounding off my hastily erected shield and circling for a different angle.

The fear in her had been overpowered by total outrage. It was yet another confirmation that I'd made the right choice, but night was coming, and I didn't have the time for sparring with a beginner. Ignoring her clumsy attempts at mental combat, I searched the memory centers of her brain, finding the training and extensive knowledge ingrained from her childhood and stint in Afghanistan. She'd been an eager and apt student.

The persistent hammering against my thoughts grew irritating. I walked Camilla's body to the empty wooden chair, the shorter legs and wider hips unbalancing me until I adjusted my stride. I lowered my new body onto Camilla's battered furniture, giving my attention to its formerly solitary tenant.

"Quiet, lieutenant!" I growled. Unfurling an arm of thought, I hooked her presence and coiled her into a wrestler's hold, pinning her mind-self into a tight ball. "You agreed to help me, without knowing the specifics of your duty. And if you will relax, I will explain." She strained against me, all teeth and flailing limbs.

Camilla's anger was fast simmering into hatred. An image of her snarling face coalesced before me, the eyes dark and fiery. I chuckled at the rebellious woman, savoring the conflict.

"What the fuck is going on?" she panted. "Who are you?" A tendril of her thoughts escaped and stung me. Growling again, I wrapped her tighter and squeezed hard. She choked, spat, and pushed back with astonishing strength.

Holding her was like trying to restrain an angry cat. I contained another newly formed tendril of her thought and felt my annoyance deepen. Very well, time to switch tactics.

"I am War, Camilla." I said it bluntly, expecting to surprise her into a double-take.

She didn't miss a beat, her angry attack becoming more effective and painful with each assay she made. "Fuck you, asshole," muttered Camilla. She rapid-fired several blows into me, trying to get enough space to get away. "If you're War, I'm the goddamn angel of death. Let me go!" The last three words were punctuated with swift jabs, followed by a final hit that sneaked past my guard. Blinded, I released her and shook myself, seeing red for more than one reason. I heard her laugh and answered her with a shattering roar that escaped into the physical and shook the dust from Camilla's windows. She reeled, faltering in her dance around me.

I dove, pinning her against the walls of our arena. Blazing, I saw myself reflected in her stunned face, the twin fires in my bony eye sockets reflected in her dark eyes. I roared again, pure rage driving me beyond words for a few moments as she twisted beneath me. She quailed, and I recovered my more civilized voice.

"Mortal woman, you cannot hope to win this," I hissed. "Yield now and you may yet get your life back."

Camilla stayed tense and straining against my hold. "You have no right—"

"I have no time." Snapping off ribbons of thought, I bound her tight before she had another opportunity to free herself. Her face rippled with dismay as she tested her bonds and found them unyielding. Expression smoothing into a mask of impassivity, she again looked directly into my own eyes, fiery though they were.

"What are you going to do with me?" Piercing and unflinching she stared at me, her fear reined in tight.

Battle rage fading into respect, I saluted her. She glared back, unrepentant and glorious.

"You'll find out soon enough, officer."

She glared. "You owe me an answer!"

Rage came charging back on the heels of a stab of shame. "I owe you nothing!" I bellowed. Camilla's hands responded to my sentiment by clenching on the arms of her wooden chair where we both sat.

Camilla weathered the onslaught of my anger as though it were a mere gust of wind and she a rock. "This is my body, you—"

I cut her off with a sharp gesture, silencing her against her will. Her face registered shock spiked with anger and fear.

"First lieutenant, you are my prisoner, until such time as I have learned all I need to know. Your fate after that point is in your own hands."

Camilla paused and then surprised me yet again by miming a sardonic laugh.

Wary now, I nodded to her and turned most of my attention back to making her body my own. I would need full control before tonight's meeting, but I had learned I couldn't afford to ignore her.

Oh god, what is happening to me?

Camilla hunkered in the back of her mind, claustrophobia squeezing her tight. It was obscene to be sharing her own head with someone else, watching someone else pull her nerves to clench fists, to stand, to touch wood and metal. It was a creepy, cobwebbed feeling. Her body shifted into a loosely coiled defensive position and bobbed and weaved to throw a quick jab at a phantom opponent. The smooth movements made the insides of her head swirl as though she were watching an IMAX movie on skydiving.

This shouldn't be happening, she thought numbly. I should be well on my way to the gym, followed by a solitary drunken weekend, not forced into the backseat of my own mind by something calling itself War.

She giggled nervously and recognized the panic that caused it. She wanted to wrap her arms around herself and rock, drain her scotch in one smoky gulp, laugh, cry—*something* to prove to herself that her body was still her own. The entire bizarre experience was beginning to feel like an extremely vivid dream, one where she couldn't move a muscle. Admittedly, this was a new twist on the usual theme.

The shadow-boxing stopped as abruptly as it had begun. Camilla's view dipped over her barren desk to watch her hands pull out and rifle through mostly empty drawers. Her car keys jangled as they were snagged from their hook and pocketed.

So what option does this leave me? she thought. Frustration and possessiveness grappled with blank terror. What can I do? Can he hear what I'm thinking? The sheer absence of privacy was humiliating.

There had to be something—shit, *anything*—she could do to regain some sort of a handle on this. Something whispered that she had never had a handle on it, and she suppressed it viciously. That was the last thing she needed right now.

The next thought struck her like a slap. I could work with him.

Her chest clenched at the thought.

Idiot. Remember your training. If you can't escape, you misdirect until you can escape. If escape is completely impossible, go along with your captor—until you can escape. And if you botch your escape, at least you will have worked against the enemy, made him dependent on you, damaged his plans with your death.

Camilla's panic was subsiding, mutating into something she remembered feeling last before she left active duty—excitement. She quashed the emotion fiercely, determined to keep her plans hidden.

I don't need to fear this, she thought fiercely. I've been a student of war my whole life. Now let's see if I can master it. Besides, those drunken weekends were becoming monotonous.

"The doc will be here in a few. Hang tight." Olivia spoke more to herself than to the suspect. Once Dorsey was secure in an interrogation room, Quinn pulled Olivia aside. She bristled and yanked her arm back.

"What? If you tell me to do paperwork or go home, I'm going to break your arm for real this time." Too harsh, but it was out and couldn't be called back. She glared back toward the box they'd put the firebug in, wondering what else the crazy had done.

"Liv," said Quinn, putting himself in her sight line. His face was lined with irritation and concern, and she just couldn't keep the fire raging with her partner in the way. She scowled and looked down.

"We're not letting him off, Liv. But if we don't call in psych and have them rule on it, that kid's lawyer is going to have a field day, once he gets one." He reached out again, and this time Olivia accepted the gesture. "If nothing else, we can make sure he doesn't get the chance to do this again."

Olivia sighed. "I know! I know." She gave him the best smile she could manage and punched him lightly on the shoulder. I'm going to call Camilla and let her know I won't be there tonight, and then we can settle in to watch the shrink show."

"There's my partner. Say hi to your girlfriend for me!"

"For fuck's sake, Quinn. Give it a rest." Back on familiar ground, Olivia threw a mock punch at his head.

Ducking, Quinn giggled like a child. "I thought the U-Haul was compulsory on the second date, anyway."

"Stop getting your information from crappy TV shows, asshole." She picked up the phone and dialed Camilla's number. The ring trilled in her ear three times and switched to voice mail.

"You've reached Camilla Sykes. Leave a message."

The girl must hate phones. Olivia had never once caught her live.

"Hey Cam, this is Liv. I caught a case and I'll be here for a while, so we should reschedule the mutual beating. Next week? Let me know." Olivia caught Quinn's sugary grin as she put the handset down and flipped him off.

He snorted, then visibly shook himself back into work mode. "The substitute shrink is on his way up."

Olivia raised her eyebrows. "That was fast."

"I know. We may want to keep his number on hand if he's any good. Name's Bill Kroner."

She leaned over to jot down the name on a spare notepad, then led the way to the elevator.

5

War Games

"Am I ready?" I whispered. I watched unfamiliar fingers clench at my command and remembered the last time I had worn a new body. The experience had been very different.

Across the room, something buzzed repeatedly and then stopped. A mobile phone, perhaps? A shudder of distaste shook my shoulders. Camilla touched my thoughts with a cleared throat sensation. I reluctantly turned my thoughts back to her, shoulders tensed.

Her demeanor had shifted. Her anger and resentment were now covered with a hard shell and barely visible. I raised an eyebrow, considered her, then dissolved her gag.

Without preamble, she demanded, "Why me?"

I blinked. "I told you the truth before, lieutenant. I need you to bring me into the present. You're a soldier and a woman, and I cannot think of a better candidate." I sensed there was more to her question and felt a red-tinged tide of irritation tug at me.

She shook off my explanation without a hitch. "I'm no one of any power. Not even the army seems to want me, and if you are what you say you are, you could have taken anyone." She snorted. "You're stealing my body like you'd steal a car and seem to think I'll go along with it like a lamb. You're out of your mind!"

That red tide was rising again. Fighting it back choked me. "I do not have time for this." I spun around to face the door, key clenched in one hand.

Camilla laughed openly now, a grating sardonic bark. "You have time to rape me in a way I didn't even think was possible, but you don't even try to explain yourself and maybe get me to help you? Wouldn't this all be easier if you didn't have to fight me every step of the way? Because really," she snarled, teeth bared, "I will fight you. And I learn quick."

I fought down the urge to slap her and considered her oblique offer. Her memories and experiences were what I had been hoping to gain, and by examining them fashion a new glass through which to view the world, but having her opinions and advice at hand could be invaluable. Especially if it meant I could have my full attention on the tasks ahead of me tonight.

I bent my head, tracing the worn metal of the key in my hand. "This is a fair request and well reasoned. Would you allow me to explain as we travel to save time?"

There was no spark of triumph flaring in her image, but I could feel it against my thoughts like the gleam on a knife's edge. "Are you going to give me my body back when you're done?"

Cooperation, I thought. "As soon as my goals are achieved." Guilt thrust at me again, and I was glad of Camilla's inexperience on this battlefield.

"Then let's get to my car," she said. "The sooner we start this, the sooner we end it."

Quiet, conscience. I collected myself and left the small room for the wider world beyond.

"So what do I call you, then? I'm not calling you 'War.' It'll just make me laugh." She sounded darkly amused even to be thinking such a question.

The sun was already behind the horizon as I trudged toward Camilla's car parked in a lot a few hundred yards ahead. I picked up my pace. My smile tugging at Camilla's lips felt sadder than I'd expected. "Call me Alexander, then." It had not been a long time since I'd thought of him, though this situation was only similar in the coarse details.

Camilla laughed and raised an incredulous eyebrow. "What, as in 'the Great'?" As though I were making a joke.

I blinked and felt the smile fall away. I shrugged off the comment and beckoned her out of her bolt-hole.

"Start your lessons, Camilla." She would know she had touched a nerve, but I couldn't afford to spend time on that subject and the history to which it would lead. Her eyes marked it, but she let it pass.

Camilla grinned, an unexpected and easy expression. "Sure, Al. And call me Cam. All my friends do."

I winced. "We're hardly friends, Camilla. At best, we are allies of circumstance." She acknowledged the point with a roll of her mental shoulders, her image still determined in my mind's eye. "I have also never liked the irreverence of shortened names, Camilla. You should tolerate hearing your full name and speaking mine." I caught her gaze and held it. "This is a business relationship, nothing more."

A ghost of her snarl flitted across her face, gone almost as quickly as it had appeared. "And I'm getting the short shaft."

The guilt was not becoming easier to control. "If this works the way I plan, I'll give you nearly anything you ask for, Camilla." Lies. Next, I would be back to playing games with the rest of my siblings. I pushed the thoughts away with an effort.

"Get on with it, then."

I let her frustration drip off me. We had no time to finish this now, though I would greatly enjoy unleashing my anger. War is neither subtle nor restrained.

The path rose before me, warming my muscles pleasantly. "I have recently suffered a significant business setback. I need to meet my associates to set it right."

Her gaze sharpened. "What kind of setback? And why do you need me?"

The woman was too sharp by half. "You are likely much more conversant with military arms than the average person."

"Excuse me?"

Explanations, exposition—I didn't want to discuss it. The more I looked back at today's events, the less I wanted to consider them. "I was fooled into destroying my last identity and need to grasp the reins of my business before it escapes completely."

Her brow furrowed as I crested a hill. "Who the hell could fool you into anything? And what business?" She paused, and her look darkened into a cold glare. "Are you a freaking arms dealer?"

I stiffened. "I sell that which I have always sold. And—"

She cut me off, her face stark and righteous as an angel's. "What the hell, Alexander! I'm not helping you steal weapons from the US military. Never in a million years would I be willing to do that. Who do you think I am? A traitor?" She was burning with her fury, with eyes sparking.

"Be still, lieutenant!" I barked, cutting her off in turn. "I am an honorable man. I do not steal, nor will I force you to do so."

Camilla barely staggered even from the heat of my rage. "Then what?"

I picked up my pace, forcing my short strides to eat up the hill. "In this particular instance, I merely need a new body. Your other talents will be of use later."

She growled. "Goddamn war crow."

I did not deign to respond. Finally cresting the hill, I took us across the empty lot to her car.

"Where are we going?" she demanded. The dangerous growl had not left her voice.

I had no time to correct her grudging attitude. "Storm King State Park. As I said, I have a meeting." No time and barely a ghost of a plan.

The night was brisk, wind coming in off the Hudson River in the distance. Camilla's car was a flat black 1962 Ford Mustang. The thrill I'd felt earlier at finding her memory of it came back. It lightened my mood enough to tug one corner of my mouth up. It pleased me that Camilla obviously did not aim for safety or security with her vehicle.

I unlocked it and settled into the curved leather seat, a post-factory racing style addition to the old car. Responding to my questioning thought, Camilla stirred and muttered, "State law, had to upgrade the seat belts."

That actually surprised a laugh out of me. I started the car, and the engine roared like an angry lion.

Putting the transmission into gear, we pulled out of the lot and headed toward the gatekeeper and the open road.

"What the hell is this guy doing?" muttered Quinn as he paced behind the one-way glass. Olivia ignored him, her arms wrapped tightly around her body. He had a point, but the pacing was distracting.

The new psych guy had sounded competent, with a soft accent and bright eyes. He'd taken a cursory look at the firebug's medical file, nodding absently as the three of them walked and talked their way back to the holding room. Without even a glance to show he'd understood, Kroner had waved them into the observation room and let himself in with Dorsey.

The new room they'd put him in was much quieter and almost completely empty. Ian took one shaky breath, then another. The angry voices in his head had turned down the volume to almost nothing, as close as they had come in hours to leaving him.

He sneaked a glance at the man sitting across from him. He was small and unassuming, his suit neat to a fault, a completely bland navy. His hair was sandy blond, cropped close to a well-shaped skull. The only arresting feature this man had were his eyes—a brilliant, witchy green.

The man's expression sharpened when Ian's gaze caught on those eyes. Ian felt a sparkle of guilt and excitement shoot through him.

Shit, he saw me gawking!

"Are you Ian Dorsey?" asked the man quietly. His voice was softly accented with an exotic flavor.

Wincing and casting his gaze to the floor, Ian nodded. He noticed with vague surprise that the handcuffs were gone from his wrists. He lifted his left hand and turned it over to look at the red mark the metal had left.

The man leaned forward abruptly, bringing Ian's attention back to him with a snap.

Like a rubber band, thought Ian, Crack!

He wanted to think more about that, but the lovely voice was speaking again.

"My name is Bill Kroner, Mr. Dorsey." He opened a fat manila folder sitting on the table between them. "I'm a doctor, and I'm here to help you."

Ian pulled away from the medical file open in front of him. He lifted his right thumb to his mouth to bite the nail. "I don't think you're here to help me, Bill. I think you're here to help the police frame me for my father's death."

Smart boy!

He's smarter than he looks.

Bill gave him a steady look and a soft smile. The eyes, though, were still rock hard.

"Ian, I can assure you that I'm not here for the police. In fact, the police would rather I wasn't here."

Liar.

"Liar! I heard that big beefy cop call for the doc. That's you. You're here to help them. I'm crazy, not stupid!" Ian spat out a piece of nail onto the table. It was bloody and he ignored it so he could start on the left thumb.

Bill's hard eyes searched his face for a moment, and Ian squirmed in his chair. "Honestly, Mr. Dorsey, you can trust me. I'm not even the regular police psychiatrist. You are my agenda, not the police or their motives." The ugly room was silent for a few moments.

The unremarkable face turned inward, and Bill sat back into his chair with a sigh. "You couldn't be simple and cooperative just to give me a hand, could you?" The well-manicured hands scrubbed over his bland face, which had fallen into weary lines.

Ian looked at him obliquely, his teeth frozen halfway through the last bit of nail.

Maybe he could help you.

With a jerk, Ian ripped the last bit of white nail from his thumb. No blood in his mouth this time—a good omen.

"What the hell, why not?" said Ian, the nail still clenched between his teeth. He spat it at the table to join its brother and stood abruptly to brace his arms on the table, leaning over Bill. "What do you think you can help me with?"

Bill hadn't even blinked at Ian's jerky movements. "You mentioned the name of the client you sent up to your father's office today. Who was it again?" There was a false nonchalance in his soft voice. Ian crowed inwardly to know he had something the doctor wanted.

Can't deal if you don't have something to barter, Ian!

"What do I get if I tell you?" The voices purred at his cleverness.

Bill shook his head. "And you said you were smart, Ian. The cops told me what you said already. I just need it confirmed." Swiftly, Bill stood to stand close to Ian, his mouth at Ian's ear. "And once it's confirmed," he whispered, "I'll help you find him. That's what you really want, isn't it?"

Smooth skin pressed against Ian's unshaven cheek. The connection bit and stung in a way that had nothing to do pain and Ian nodded, breathing in fast gasps. He turned his own mouth to Bill's ear and whispered, "Mr. Alexander Sekhmet."

There was a loaded pause, and Ian felt Bill smile against his neck. "There you are, that wasn't hard, was it?" He reached down to pat Ian's hand lingeringly. He drew back and sat down again, motioning Ian to do the same.

Still breathing hard, Ian stayed on his feet. "You'll do what you said?" If he had still had long thumbnails, they would have been drawing blood from his palms. Bill gestured at the chair again, and Ian sat, awkward and unsure.

"Ian, we want the same thing. I need to get you released from this place first. Then I'll do exactly as I said." His expression had returned to the mild, bland face he'd shown before, but his eyes were lit as if from within.

Green sparklers. Fireworks!

This man would help him. Even the voices believed that.

And if he's lying somehow, thought Ian, he's next on the list.

A chorus of approving whispers swept through him.

"Camilla? You are unusually quiet."

The Hudson rippled like dark silk on their left, the trees to their right like a bristling wall. Camilla didn't once feel a need to chide Alexander for his driving, and it was getting to her.

"Camilla," he said finally, "what is it?"

She sighed explosively and wondered vaguely how she could do that without a body. "Good lord, do you have to drive like an old man? You're actually below the speed limit."

Alexander laughed and she shivered. Somehow he twisted her voice into something dark and menacing even when he expressed amusement.

"Understand, Camilla, I haven't survived as long as I have by being reckless." He shifted in the cradle of the driver's seat.

"I always thought a certain amount of recklessness was necessary in times of war." Survived?

Alexander shook his (her!) head slowly. "You are right, but you must pick those moments, choose them carefully like succulent sweets. Too much abandon and your enemy will have your head above the gates."

Camilla snorted. "You don't sound like a tactician; you sound like a history professor."

"They are not mutually exclusive."

Oh man, she ached to push the accelerator down, to throw something, anything, her impatience boiling over. "And what do you mean by 'I haven't survived this long'? I wouldn't have thought War would need to worry about survival. Humans fighting each other over disagreements is never going to go away." Camilla could see Alexander clench his hands (her hands? Their hands?) tightly on the black, leather-wrapped steering wheel. Another sore spot, she thought.

Alexander relaxed with effort. Camilla could still feel the blood rushing back into those pale fingers. "You have a family, do you not? Friends, allies?"

"What? Of course I do," she retorted.

"So do I. My Family members are the only ones who can hurt me. And they are all old enough that their duties seem to have lost their savors, and they've turned to other games." Alexander took a deep breath and let it out slowly. "I cannot help but suspect that my current position can be traced back to a bored sister or brother."

Camilla winced in unexpected sympathy. "I'm not close to my family either. I haven't been home since my active duty was over." She let out a dry laugh. "I talk more with the people I box with at the gym."

"Comrades in arms are much more trustworthy, I agree."

She felt a tightness in her chest and squashed it, hard. "I suppose you would know, War. Are we going to run into these crazies? A drunken Thor, or a pissed off giant spider?"

Alexander straightened his shoulders. "Camilla, I will discuss all of this with you later, I promise. I do not have enough time for explanations at this point. This meeting is critical to the survival you mentioned. Must I state that your survival is tied directly to mine?"

About to let her tongue loose, Camilla stopped to consider his words. Did he really mean that he—that War—could die? That she would die with him?

Punctiliously, Alexander flipped the Mustang's blinker on and curved gently onto a gravel road, barred several feet up by a large gate that posted the hours for the state park. Alexander didn't slow as he approached the obviously chained and locked gate.

"Alexander? What're you—HEY!" She scrambled for the controls to her body, panic kicking in. He seemed to expect it and pushed her away with ease. She fell back, gaze pinned on the gate her beautiful car was about to hit.

Then, with a gesture that Camilla more felt than saw, Alexander unlocked and swept open the gate. Gravel flew as the car growled between the posts, and while Camilla couldn't turn to watch, she felt sure the gate had swung shut behind them in the same fashion. Anger flared.

"You could have told me, you bastard! What was that, you proving you could still scare me? Pointlessly fucking mean, if you ask me!" Camilla really, really wanted to punch Al in the face, even if she ended up breaking her own damn nose.

War was laughing again, a rich sound that still sounded like it was constructed from the screams of the dying. "I wished to show you two things, Camilla. One, that I am quite capable of many things, including callousness to my acquaintances. Two, that I am in control—not you." He shrugged nonchalantly, still smiling. "I could have blown this car to its component atoms, and we would have walked away unscathed."

Camilla spat out, "So what, are you like Houdini then? Someone can punch you in the gut, and as long as you're braced for it, you're golden, but if you're not ready, you'll bleed to death? Sounds like a crappy life to me."

Alexander had returned to his former elderly driving and took an infuriating moment to respond.

"I do not fear you or your fellow mortals, not at all. Only my Family has that kind of power, the strength required to break the treaty and kill one of the gods. Young woman, this is not your life. This is a few days of your life, imposed on by mine. You are in no place to judge me or the laws by which I must abide to survive." He wrapped his fingers around the gear shifter, pushed it smoothly into third. More gravel spun out from under the wheels as they sped up. "And it is not merely my own existence that concerns me in this. If War were to become war—that is to say, a human war, ruled by humanity's cruelty and capricious nature—your species would not long outlive me."

She shook her whirling head, trying to parse what Alexander was saying. "What are you talking about? Goddamn metaphysical crap—"

He rode over her, words implacable. "Do you honestly think your species would have survived nuclear weapons without my influence? Mutually assured destruction didn't keep your leaders from pushing that button. I did." His smile brittle and sharp, he said, "My purpose is War, not the end of wars."

Camilla was still. Looking away, she muttered, "Let's just get this over with."

Bill nodded to Ian once, sharp as a punch, then levered himself to his feet. Ian went to work on the nail of his right index finger, worrying at the difficulty of getting himself out of this mess. He looked up when Bill touched his shoulder.

"Stay here. I'll be back for you in just a moment." He smiled, his eyes still bright, and left the room, shutting the door carefully behind him.

Dorsey and Kroner were standing on opposite sides of the table, leaning together, cheeks close as lovers. Olivia's frown eased some as they stepped back.

"You'll do what you said?" Dorsey's voice was tinny over the small speaker.

"Shit, now what? Good thing he doesn't have a lawyer present."

"Shh!"

"I need to get you released from this place; then, I'll do exactly as I said."

No. "No. No way is that happening." Olivia pushed away from the wall, ready to read newbie shrink the riot act.

"Olivia. I've got this." Quinn pushed past her and out the door, shutting it behind him. She stopped short at the closed door, furious. Damn him. Damn men.

Fingers digging into her biceps, Olivia turned back to their suspect, anger banking down as she tried to make sense of his behavior.

Ian stared after Bill for a protracted moment, caught.

What's he doing? He's coming back for us, right?

A faint echo of Bill's voice came through the solid metal door, indecipherable and curiously flat. Far off in the back of Ian's mind, a quiet alarm bell began to ring. Can I really trust this guy?

The voices erupted in a rush of condemnation.
Ian, don't mess this up!
He's the only one who believes you.
Don't you dare fuck this up.
Or you'll pay.
Ian cringed at the barrage, ducking down against the table and gnawing furiously on his fingernail.
"I won't!" he whispered, eyes shut tight. "I promise, I'm sorry!" He used the moment to creep up to the one-way mirror, leaning his head against the wall in an attempt to hear what was going on.
An odd sound from the real world cut into the tirade and his apologies—a sound like two arrows hitting a target: thunk-thunk. The door rattled.

Dorsey was leaning against the wall, chewing his nails madly and muttering to himself. Outside, something rattled and thumped twice. A stray thought interpreted the noise as Quinn getting his point across. She smiled grimly.
Then two sharp bangs sounded, coming from the office proper. Olivia looked up, the suspect forgotten.
Flash-bang grenades? What the hell?

Seconds later, the door flew open and Bill rushed into the interrogation room, his face intent and predatory. Outside, there were two more percussive bangs, much sharper, followed by faint shouts.
Bill grabbed Ian by the wrist and dragged him through the door and around the still form of a man lying in a pool of blood.
That's the cop! He killed the cop!

When Olivia turned back, the suspect was gone.
"Fuck!"
Olivia sprang for the door to find the way blocked by Quinn, his heavy shape prone in front of the doorway. The door itself was covered with blood spatter.

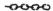

He's helping us, I knew he would!

Bill swiftly guided him around the still bodies of other cops and abandoned upturned furniture until they reached the exit.

Who is this guy? Can we really trust him?

Shut up, don't you dare ruin this!

They passed a scorched cylinder on the floor, smoke still trickling from one end. Ian took a deep breath of cold night air as the door finally shut behind them. Freedom was good, so good. It didn't matter how he got out. It didn't.

Bill yanked him down a dark alley, and Ian followed.

Olivia went cold. "No, no, no . . ." The word tumbled from her in a never-ending stream, as if she could fix Quinn with denial. She shoved her hand into his bloody shirt front, fingers searching for a pulse that wasn't there.

She sucked in a shocked breath and coughed hard. Smoke was billowing through the hallways like a bank of fog, triggering a flashed memory of her mother during the house fire. Familiar voices shouted in fear and pain.

Kroner. It had to be Kroner; Quinn had left to talk with him, and the suspect had been safely in the room. She leaned over to check; Quinn's service pistol was still at his hip, but they hadn't bothered to search Kroner on his arrival.

Clenching her bloodied fists, Olivia stepped over the body of her partner and dove into the smoke and mayhem beyond.

"Wherever we're going, I really hope we get there soon. I'm going to jump out of my skin at this rate." For a sullen, solitary woman, Camilla had much to comment on. When I didn't respond, she huffed and turned away from me. Silence, finally.

The road moved from drifts of gravel to rutted dirt with still a mile to my usual meeting place. The timing was close to my original plan, though I might have been even earlier. I always arrived early. I never truly knew when an associate would become a problem, as yesterday's events made painfully clear.

With a hitch in my step, I wondered what Apollo had actually seen of my troubles this morning. My brother-cousin's mind was clear as smoked glass. Had he even seen anything?

The thought brought a dramatic sense memory. Pushing aside the delicious vision of Dorsey's head cleft from his shoulders in an arcing spray of bright blood, I shook my head and pulled Camilla's Mustang to a halt in a bower made of pine boughs and sharp bushes. It was unlikely to be found at this distance, and I had previously always arrived on foot. I emerged from the car into a thicket of nettles, spiny and bristled. In the back of our shared mind, Camilla stirred and protested, declaring that even if I were uncaring of the state of her body, she surely was not.

Of course, she did not use those precise words.

I did not respond verbally, but lifted the hands I had used to push my way through the nettles, giving Camilla a close view of her own, unmarked flesh. She subsided, voice weary.

She does not trust me, I thought. Another point in her favor.

The walk was not long, a mere half-mile. Camilla's young, springy muscles were well up to the task, and we made good time. The clearing resolving at the end of the path housed a small, dark cabin. I crept up to the rough stone walls. All was quiet and bathed in bright moonlight. The nocturnal forest creatures made their way around me in unconcerned arcs. Camilla's attention was caught by the form of a bear, lumbering mere feet away. I touched her thoughts, thinking she might be frightened. When I instead touched raw wonder, I pulled back as though burned.

It had been a very long time since I had touched wonder, even longer since I had felt the emotion myself. I was taken aback by my instinctive reaction and sorrowed by it.

We all lost something in this divinity. I had not thought to be hurt by the presence of a thing I lacked.

Stung, I pulled her away from the animals of the dark wood and approached the cabin door. It was steel, probably an unusual choice for a rustic hut in a state park. I touched the metal and smiled as it recognized me, leaning into my touch like a well-loved hound. Steel was not my tool; it was more nearly my pet, my child. I caressed the slick surface and the metal opened, singing. Camilla heard nothing; her self was still too separate from mine. It would be days before we could hear each other without effort. And by then, I hoped she would not care.

The interior of the one-room cabin was pitch black, for I had long ago walled up the windows and sealed every crack. Nothing short of a nuclear warhead would break this bunker. I extended my senses, both Camilla's physical and my mental powers. The room was cool and devoid of life, the furnishings and host-gifts undisturbed since my last meeting. At my approval, the door swung shut behind me and locked with a soft click.

Camilla broke into my thoughts. "Maybe you can see, oh spirit of war, but to me it's pretty fucking dark in here. Could you hit the lights or something?"

She was fidgeting and on edge. My hands wanted to writhe under the weight of her discomfort.

I walked unerringly to the large rough-hewn table I had set in the center of the cabin and found the box of matches I had left there next to the hurricane lamp. I struck a match and watched the flame settle, then lit the lamp, setting the paned glass back over it. Camilla reached forward again to tap my thoughts with her own.

"Alexander, why can you see in the dark with my eyes, and I can't?"

I sighed, hands gripping the rough edge of the table. "I do not have answers for everything, Camilla. I apologize. I am under some measure of stress."

She paused, as though weighing my reaction. I wondered how much of the concern in her mind was for me. "Don't worry about it, Alexander. One step at a time. I hope you know what you're doing, at least. I sure don't." Her tone was wry.

I repressed a chuckle. I was alarmed to find myself wishing that I could have known her without needing to be her captor.

Shaking off the unwelcome feeling, I went back to arranging the cabin to my liking. I lit the fire in the fireplace, moved the five chairs I would need on either side of my own position at the head of the table, facing the door. I brought out six wine goblets and a bottle of dark merlot, then settled myself into the rock-hard walnut chair and waited.

After a few minutes, Camilla began fidgeting again. This woman did not have an iota more of patience than was required to live through one day at a time.

"When are these people supposed to be here?"

I sniffed the air, questioned the bear still bulldogging through the woods. "Perhaps thirty minutes."

Camilla sent me an exasperated sigh. "For chrissake Alexander, we got here almost an hour ago."

"I know." I shifted minutely in my chair, which had not been made to Camilla's measurements. "But the meeting time on which we agreed is nearly an hour away. I prefer to be more prepared than my associates."

"So you don't trust them?"

I thought of Hertzog Kroner, his stone face and flickering eyes.

"No. I do not."

Chuckling, undeterred by my cold tone, Camilla responded, "And I suppose he outmans you every time, is irritated by you arriving first, and tries to follow you home, too."

I raised my eyebrows, surprised. "That is true."

"Are you the seller or the buyer?"

"Today I sell, tomorrow I may buy. My side of the deal doesn't matter, only the deal itself."

"Here's where you could actually use some advice. Information would get you a better paycheck. And an easier handle on your associates." How dare this child condescend to me? I bristled.

Before I could rebut her argument, Camilla cut me off. "Trust me. Arms dealers are on the lower end of the food chain these days. If you sold information, these morons would treat you a lot better."

I took a moment to restrain myself and was about to respond when the bear scented a car on its way up the path. "We will deal with that later, Camilla. They are here now." I considered her words again. "Keep your eyes on Hertzog, Camilla. Tell me what you see in him, give me a running commentary."

Camilla bared her teeth. "I can do that."

I settled back again, listening to dirt spin under expensive tires through the ears of a passing barn owl.

What I heard next was not what I'd expected.

"We're nearly there, Ian. We should talk."

They'd been in the car for a long time, Bill murmuring soothing noises as the night swept by. Ian watched the blur of dark greens solidify into leaves and bushes as Bill's car rolled to a quiet stop. Turning his head to see all of the colors mesh together again was fascinating, the world turning into an impressionist painting seen too close. A stab of disquiet pierced the haze in his mind.

I don't think I've been off my meds for this long since undergrad, he muttered to the voices. The answer was a susurrus of sliding, hushed affirmation.

Ian felt a soft touch on his shoulder. He looked up to see Bill's face wavering in the moonlight. He gripped Ian's shoulder in what may have been meant as reassurance. Ian was beginning to have a hard time deciphering what was going on outside the confines of his head.

"We'll wait here," Bill said, so quietly that Ian could barely hear him. "Once my father arrives, we'll go out to meet him. Then you'll have your chance at Mr. Sekhmet." He grinned, perfect teeth flashing.

The name set off a gong in Ian's mind, calling all the voices to the forefront, resolving into a chorus of loud anger.

The man who killed your father!

You must redeem yourself, Ian.

Bathe in his blood, in his fear.

You know what you need to do, now!

Ian twitched violently at the onslaught, pulling away from Bill's hand in the process. A confused frown flitted over that smeary face and vanished. He wondered if he could catch that expression, make it explain what was going on.

Breathing heavily, Ian reached out and grabbed Bill's hand, feeling the skin over his knuckles stretch tight. "Is he here now? I can't wait for your father, Bill,"

I can't wait. I might not be able to think straight for much longer.

"I have to see him now!" Ian was vaguely aware that his voice was getting louder, Bill's eyes getting wider.

"Ian!" hissed Bill. His eyes went icy, chips of emerald in a frozen face. Bill twisted his trapped hand, and abruptly Ian was the one trapped, his hand bent back and pinned against his chest. The move slammed Ian back against the car door. Bill's thumb pressed down hard on a nerve bundle in Ian's wrist, sending pain shooting up his arm and neck to explode into fireworks in his head. For a few seconds, Ian could see purple spots floating in the air. He yelled and tried to yank his arm back. Bill could have turned to stone in that position, for all the good Ian's struggling did.

"Let me go, let me go, lemme go, lemmego!" Ian was babbling in terror again, just like back at the police station. He started to thrash around in the car, trying to get away. His free arm smacked hard into the rear view mirror, tearing it off the windshield with a pop.

Abruptly, the pressure relaxed, and Bill let go. Ian finally found the door handle and practically fell out of the car, intending to run until he couldn't run anymore. Instead he landed in a patch of something that burned, needles poking and stinging exposed flesh. He shrieked, his skin on fire.

Is something attacking us?

Ian!

He floundered helpless for a few seconds, then Ian felt hands grab his shoulders to pull him from the acid clutches of the plants. Were they nettles? He stopped yelling and collapsed, panting heavily in Bill's flushed face. His expression was torn between anger and fear.

"Ian, please be quiet," Bill whispered as his fingers dug into Ian's shoulders. "Sekhmet was always early to my father's meetings, always well prepared, and aware of everyone who arrived. Even if my father arrived with twice the number of men he'd brought the week before, Sekhmet always had the right number of place settings, even knew the names of men he'd never met." Bill sighed, his face now twisted in regret. "I'm sure he knows now that we're here, but I don't want to take any more chances."

Swallowing hard, Ian nodded. The voices are not always right, and they're never patient. Just listen to Bill for a little while longer. Ian shrugged his shoulders by way of acknowledgment and gently closed his fingers around Bill's. It hurt, and he pulled back much more quickly, dimly realizing that something was digging further into his skin. Ian cursed silently and held up his hands to see a sparse fur of nettle spines standing out from fingernails to wrists.

Bill glanced down, too, and his face softened. He dug into his blazer and pulled a pair of tweezers from a small black velvet case. Delicately, Bill began pulling the hair-thin nettle tines. Ian watched, mesmerized by the methodical, quick movements of pluck and discard, search for the next and begin again. The air was chill, but Bill's hands were warm. He chuckled as he worked, his hands steady.

"This will give us something to do while we wait, right?" He stroked his left thumb over the newly cleared palm of Ian's hand. The wicked green of his eyes sparkled.

As the warmth of Bill's hands turned into a distracting tingle, Ian smiled, the voices murmuring encouragement in his head.

I withdrew from the owl in a rush, frowning. Ian Dorsey, unbalanced and bent on finding me, brought here and cared for by Wilhelm Kroner, a man I had met only once and had not expected to see again. I rested my chin on my hands. The number of crucial details I seemed to be missing lately was deeply disturbing.

Yet another reason I desperately needed help from Camilla. I quelled an urge to slam my fist into the table.

She stirred within me, seeming to sense my unease. "Problems?" she asked, in that practical tone that so raised my hackles. I did not like being dependent on anyone, least of all a mortal woman.

"Certainly something odd, Camilla," I responded, stretching to keep my annoyance from my thought, "Our visitors are not the men I expected to see tonight."

She paused to consider, then asked, "Are these people following you or the people you're meeting?"

I sat back in my chair. "Potentially both. One is the recently disgraced son of my associate. The other . . . the other may have witnessed me killing his father this morning."

"What?!" Camilla's shocked tone was piercing even still within the skull. I shook my head to remove some of the echo. "You killed someone today?

Who? Why?" I paused to weigh my words, and she broke in. "I need to know what you've gotten both of us into."

I rolled some tension from my shoulders, aware that I wanted to respond like a guilty child. Perhaps she did deserve some sort of explanation. I straightened and stood to set out two more goblets at the table. "He was my lawyer. I had perhaps retained him for too long. Dorsey had decided that I was some sort of demon. I do not know how he came to this conclusion, but he was privy to all of my records and dealings." I pulled two chairs up to the new place settings and resettled myself in my own chair. "I am more than human, but I am not omnipotent. I could not make him forget. I could not stop time and remove all trace of myself from his business." One corner of my mouth turned up in a sideways grin. "As I am sure you know, War has never moved secretly when the problem can be dealt with on the edge of a sword."

She glared at me, chin jutting obstinately. "Sounds more like murder than war, Alexander. How did you kill him?" Camilla's thought was insistent.

She did need to see this at some point to avoid an uproar at the wrong moment. I raised my right hand and drew my sword. It shimmered into being as I brought it into view, a Roman gladius, the edges smoking as I swept it through the air. The smell of ozone followed its path. Camilla's drop-jawed awe was extremely satisfying. "I cut his head from his shoulders and set fire to his office to hide the manner of death," I said matter-of-factly. "The only other person in the building was Ian Dorsey, my lawyer's son. I had thought him already well out of the building, but if he had hidden himself well, he may have seen me leave unscathed."

Camilla's eyes narrowed, and she lashed out, "Are you an idiot all of the time or just today?"

My grip on the sword spasmed tight. "What?!" The woman needed to learn respect for her elders. I would slap even a Family member for such a tone.

"You 'thought' he was gone. He 'may have' seen you leave a burning building without a mark on you. Not to mention that you kept all of your records with one lawyer."

I found that I had no riposte for her recriminations. I clenched my jaw, hearing Camilla's molars creak. She was right. I had been careless to an extreme, though that did not make her chiding easier to swallow.

"Now calm your ass down, Alexander, I think the universe cut you a break today. This kid is not going to recognize you in my body, and I'm betting Disgraced Son out there thinks getting rid of you could get him back into his father's good graces. We'll get through this meeting just fine." She paused and said with a luscious grin, "But I will be giving you a lecture afterward."

I searched the maple-plated ceiling of my cabin, wondering what I had brought on myself with this partnership.

As I sat with my head tipped back, another car approached, this one large and armor-plated. The owl again flew recognizance for me, dipping low as the vehicle's doors opened. The five men I expected emerged, plus one. I chuckled fondly as I set out yet another glass for the unexpected guest.

"Does it start now, for real?" Camilla sounded tense but excited. She seemed to think she was ready for anything. I hoped she was right. Oh, hells. I needed her to be right.

I settled back into my chair once more, watching the show outside.

"Bill? Can we go in now?"

"Not yet. Shh."

Seen through the owl's wide-stretched pupils, the forest was a bright and granulated wash of grays. The avian head cocked to one side, catching conversation and nuance with ears designed to hear a mouse scrabble over leaves. When the sleek black BMW eased to a halt and Kroner and his men got out, Ian's face went slack and his fingers pressed hard against his temples. Beside him, Wilhelm slid his manicure case into his jacket and pushed himself up like a mechanical doll to pace forward into the headlights, his hands motionless and above his head.

Five of the new men were huge, their suits straining at the seams. As soon as Wilhelm moved, they had handguns trained on him, their faces remote and professional. Four pointed at Wilhelm, and one heavy semi-automatic aimed directly at Ian's face. The boy swallowed hard.

Wilhelm, well aware of his father's opinion and obviously prepared for the reaction, stopped immediately and spoke clearly in harsh, musical Afrikaans. "Father," he called out, "I have something you need. Something the family needs! Please listen." His voice was compelling, almost desperate.

Hertzog Kroner, a near double of his son, paced forward to meet him. He waved the guards back with one lazy hand. "Wilhelm, my son. What do you think you're doing with this grandstanding, eh? My decision has been made. I have no reason to return you to my fold." The old man's face was stony, expressionless.

Back in the shadows, Ian clenched his long fingers about his skull, subvocalized words fluttering from his lips. The behavior plucked at deep-buried strings in my being, and my fists clenched tighter. What did he remind me of?

Wilhelm kept his hands in the air without even a twitch downward. "I believe I have found you a reason, Father, one that will redeem me in your eyes and perhaps save you from a terrible fate."

Kroner's dark green eyes narrowed, then he nodded, a barely perceptible lift of the chin. Wilhelm recognized the gesture as faint approval and lowered his hands, keeping them clearly visible and away from his sides. Staying almost perfectly still, he turned his head to one side and called out in English, "Ian, please come to me, slowly."

The boy hung back, unsure. When the gun still pointed at him waved impatiently, Ian jumped and scuttled over to hide behind Wilhelm's shoulder. Hertzog's eyes went dark.

"Wilhelm," he said, his voice harsh, wrapping around the English words like gravel, "this does not renew my faith in you."

Wilhelm's twitch was nearly invisible. "Father, this is not what you think. Ian Dorsey is the son of Mr. Sekhmet's lawyer."

At the sound of my name, Ian whipped his head up to stare at Wilhelm. Anticipation tightened every line of him.

Brow furrowing, Hertzog looked him up and down. Ian hunched his shoulders and looked away again, fidgeting. Hertzog snorted derisively.

"How is that useful to me?" His voice was arctic and angry. "I will need more than a frightened boy to take down Sekhmet, much as I'd like to."

Ian swiveled back to Kroner, nostrils flared. Words bubbled out of him, pushed and shoved by some strong emotion. "He killed my father. I saw it! He's a monster, Dad didn't even do anything."

Wilhelm cut him off hurriedly, a hand on Ian's sleeve. "You can't trust him, Father. If he's killing off his associates, you are likely next on his list." He took a breath. "Now, you're forewarned."

Hertzog took that in, and a smile crept across his face. "Ah, my son, perhaps you do have something to redeem yourself with, after all." He gestured to his guards, who put their guns away and took position around all three of them.

"Come with me to the meeting, Wilhelm. Ian as well." Hertzog laughed, deep and guttural. "I would love to set my friend Mr. Sekhmet at ease with a familiar face."

Of course he would.

His breath coming quick and shallow, Wilhelm steered Ian a respectful distance behind Hertzog. Ian's eyes rolled back and forth, a tall guard at his back looming silent and large.

"Camilla, please calm down."

I sat relaxed in my uncomfortable wooden throne, fingers curled gently over the knobbed crow's feet at the ends of the arms.

"You calm down. I've been in combat before. I'll be fine."

Camilla squirmed with impatience and excitement. Despite her fear, the woman seemed to be actually enjoying this experience.

Dismissing her mental state, I checked my body position. Slight amusement on my face, a careful slouch to indicate indifference to the gravity of the situation, chair pushed back just enough that I could stand quickly if need arose: I was ready.

When the knock finally came, Camilla would have leaped from the seat in a jolt; I simply raised one hand and motioned the door open. The steel sent a purr back to me, one I realized Camilla could just barely feel. She felt the steel. I pushed the disturbing thought aside.

A tall and muscled shape entered warily, obviously a bodyguard. His gaze swept the small cabin from one corner to the next. Then his eyes crossed mine, and immediately the man jerked into high alert and put hand to the grip of what looked like a fairly high-caliber gun tucked into a shoulder holster.

"Oh jeezus, it's Dirty Harry," Camilla thought dryly to me, "and he really wants to take out that gun and make a mess of us." Her mind buzzed with plans to knock the table over as a barrier, get me to draw my sword again. . . .

"Camilla, please. I have done this before, and I'm good at it." I waved her back, focused on the bodyguard. Frustrated, Camilla subsided into watchful grumbling silence.

Nostrils flaring, the bodyguard yelled back over his shoulder. "Clear, but take care. Sekhmet isn't here. Someone else is here, a woman."

Camilla furrowed her brow. "South Africa?" My affirmation was wordless and irritated. Camilla restrained herself again.

The first bodyguard's carbon copy came in, his gun preceding him, and was followed by the much younger figure of Wilhelm Kroner, the military cut of his blond hair glittering in the lamplight. He narrowed his eyes on seeing Camilla's body at the head of the table. His face was blank, concealing his surprise rather well.

His control didn't extend to his voice. "Who are you, woman? Where is Alexander Sekhmet?" His rising tones spoke for him. Kroner was very alarmed.

"Wilhelm Kroner." I said carefully. My stillness was as unnatural as it was vital. "I had not heard that your father had brought you back into the fold." My smile widened into a toothy grin, and the sight of it sent both men back a few steps. "Congratulations, I suppose."

Hertzog came into the room on the heels of my sneer. He stopped behind his guard to watch.

Wilhelm's face had gone colorless and waxy. "Who are you?" His eyes searched the room, as though my former self might be hiding under a table, playing some horrible prank. This part of the interview was going according to my plan, but we still had quite a ways to go before we were safe.

"My name is Camilla." Camilla sputtered at the use of her real name. I shushed her. "Alexander Sekhmet was my father."

Hertzog finally spoke. "I see no family resemblance, young woman."

Within me, Camilla muttered, "Me neither." I suppressed a snort.

The figure moving into the light was short, graying, and clearly in charge. The two guards immediately positioned themselves between him and Camilla's body. He waved them away impatiently, and they withdrew a few feet. Wilhelm stayed at his father's shoulder.

I barked out a laugh, and all four winced at the sound. "No resemblance at all, Herr Kroner?" The grin I now revealed almost burned on my lips, and Camilla could feel it prickling. It caught cold fire in her mind, and that made me smile even wider.

The old man regarded me stonily for a while, then called back over his shoulder. Shuffling sounds prefaced Ian as he was ushered in by three bodyguards. The final man followed and closed the door behind him.

I ignored the guards to focus on my first real glimpse of Ian. He wore a rumpled dark suit that smelled of smoke, his posture was hunched, and he bit his nails ferociously. Blood ran from one index finger. His eyes were wide, and it sounded as though he was muttering to himself. When his gazed crossed mine, there was no reaction.

Something relaxed a fraction within me. I damped my smile down to a low simmer and asked politely, "Are you Ian Dorsey?"

The young man jumped as though hit with a live wire. He pointed his trembling, bloody hand straight across the table. Camilla would have jerked back in shock, if she had been in control. Blessedly, she wasn't.

"How the hell did you get in there! You killed my father, you bastard, did you kill some random woman and take her body, is that it? How did you do it? What are you?!" Ian was almost spitting foam, suddenly upright and accusing. I froze for a second, then sized up the group's reactions and readied my own.

How in all the hells could this mortal hear my voice and know it like this? This was so clearly stinking of Family issues, something foul and unnatural I would need to investigate soon. Once this mess of a meeting was concluded, I needed to sit and think.

The stasis was broken when Wilhelm neatly placed himself between Ian and me, speaking in hushed tones and frantically shooting apologetic glances at the rest of the room. Ian seemed to be having none of it.

"Shut up, shut up Bill! You think I don't know the voice of a killer? The voice of the thing that killed my father?" Ian struggled fruitlessly, trying to get at me. "Take your hands off of me, you said I could have him, that you'd take me to him! I knew you were a liar, I knew it! The voices were wrong, you can't help me! Did you bring me here so he could kill me, too?" Ian babbled on and on, louder and louder, more and more the picture of the deranged. I let out a slow breath.

Behind the spectacle, Herzog Kroner cleared his throat authoritatively, then caught the eye of one of his guards and jerked his head in a decisive movement. Two of the guards nodded back and grasped the nearly incoherent boy by the shoulders to wrestle him outside. Wilhelm watched Ian go, gape-mouthed, and he started when one more guard put a hand to his elbow.

He turned a pleading look to his father, who shook his head and waved him away. The young man slumped and walked defeated from the room. At the last moment, before the door closed, I caught a glimpse of his eyes again. They were flaming madly.

As the door swung shut again, Camilla whispered to me, "I don't think we've seen the last of those two unless Daddy drops them in the Hudson tonight."

She was almost certainly right. Rolling my shoulder as though dislodging something unpleasant, I slipped back into the scene. "Now that the pre-meeting entertainment has passed, Herr Kroner, will you take a seat? We have quite a bit to discuss."

I kept my seat as I watched my associate look me up and down, weighing the last few minutes. He came to a decision and lowered himself into the seat across from me, at the foot of the table. Separated by several feet of heavy wood, Herzog cocked his head at me.

"Alexander Sekhmet was your father?" His dark eyes were curious, cunning. I shrugged.

"We were never close, not like most families," I said dismissively and watched his expression narrow at that. "He was killed in a fire at the office of his lawyer this morning."

Herzog showed me his own teeth in a grimace made nut brown from years of cigars. "How unlike him." A light went on behind his eyes, and his smile firmed into something genuine. "I would have expected him to be the cause of a fire, not a victim."

I shrugged again, easing into the parry and riposte of those who need but do not trust each other. "He was perhaps not the best father, but he was an excellent teacher." Camilla sputtered again within me, laughing. I tried to ignore her.

"I take it, then, Miss Sekhmet," said Herzog, leaning elbows on the table to steeple his hands, "that I am expected to deal with you from now on." The smile had dropped away, and now the businessman was in charge.

I shook my head fondly. "No Herr Kroner, my father's operation can sail or sink under its own weight, under another captain." I laid back further in the chair, awkwardly swinging my right leg over the arm. "My business is information."

Shock emanated from Camilla's thoughts. "What the hell, Alexander, I thought—"

I shushed her. Her plan was good, and I would hit the ground running with it. I had always been very comfortable with switching plans in mid-stride. "I've supplied my father for years. It's how he managed to be the best in his field."

Camilla gathered herself, mind-self shaking. "You'd better be able to listen to me then," Camilla hissed forcefully, "because this could get sticky. You don't even know what they'll be asking about!" She desperately wished for a shot of whiskey, wanted that smoky heat shooting into her stomach to center her.

"No whiskey, Camilla, but we do have wine." I reached forward and brought the glass of merlot to my lips. I took a minute sip, rolling the flavors around my mouth.

"Great. Of course you're a wine snob." Amusement flared as I swallowed and set the glass down.

Still slouched in the chair like an insolent teenager, I raised an eyebrow at my guests. "Well?"

Herzog had been staring steadily at me, calculating. At the question, he took a breath and sighed theatrically. "My dear girl, the only information I require from you is the name of your father's second in command. I have my own network. I trust it far more than I trust you."

"Jesus. Do you even have a second?" I quieted her again, giving her an inward smile.

I would clearly need to send word to Asag, once this meeting concluded. I leaned forward, copying Herzog's earlier pose. "That I will give you free of charge. And perhaps a small snippet of my wares, to show their worth?" I felt in the inner pocket of my long coat, pulled out my second's card, wrote upon the back with a thought, and tossed it across the table. "I suggest you deal with Asag only by phone, as his physical presence is unpleasant, to put it mildly." One of the guards slapped the card to a stop and picked it up to hand over to Kroner.

Nodding first at the printed information on the front of the card, Kroner turned it over and frowned. He shot a sharp glance up to me and barked a command to the guard behind him who handed over a small cellular phone. Kroner pushed one button and brought the phone to his ear. We could hear the ring from across the table—the double pulse of an international call.

Waiting for the connection to go through, Kroner demanded, "Are you certain of this information?"

I dipped a small nod at him. "Completely."

The call was picked up with an audible click and the tinny sound of an unintelligible voice on the other end. Kroner cut it short with a rattling stream of Afrikaans, the words sounding fast and sharp.

I leaned back in the chair again as the conversation went back and forth. Lifting my wine glass again, I politely looked away from the phone call.

"What's going on? Can you understand him?" Camilla was itching to know what Kroner was saying. The tone of his voice was rushed and irritated, exactly as I wanted it. "What was on that card?"

"I told him that his brother had planted a bomb in his car back in Johannesburg." Smiling slightly, I brought the glass up to take in the aroma of the wine.

Camilla paused, dumbstruck. "Fuck, is that true? How do you know?"

I took the smallest of sips and grinned at her moan of annoyance. Obviously, the subtleties of wine were of no interest to Camilla. "I know because I sold the bomb to the younger Mr. Kroner."

Camilla blinked. "Okay. I can see this family isn't exactly tight." She paused and asked, "What was that with the son, anyway?"

I shook my head slightly, my grip on the wine glass tightening. "The young man is a homosexual, and Herzog does not approve."

Camilla frowned. "Lovely."

Interesting. "You think less of him for this? I had thought, with your position—"

Cutting me off, Camilla growled, "Oh, just shut up. You don't treat family that way. And besides, it's wasteful. You use what you have, you don't toss it away because it doesn't fit your outdated expectations."

Camilla gauged my interest and dodged away from further analysis. "So what's he doing, confirming your information?"

"Yes," I responded distractedly. I listened for a moment, my inward smile growing. "His driver has been sent away from the car, and his people are going over the engine right now. And—yes, they found it." I took another sip of wine to hide the smile that had crept out to my lips.

Across the room, a tiny uproar was brewing. Kroner was spitting angry words into the phone, and the guards were exchanging concerned looks. One guard muttered to another, who quietly left the cabin. Camilla thought that he was probably off to check their own car.

I heard the thought. "Right again. Though it is unlikely they will find anything. Herzog's men have always been very thorough."

Camilla snorted, and I covered another vulpine smile. Obviously, they were not thorough enough.

Shutting the clamshell phone with a snap, Kroner looked up, his face flushed and angry. "How did you know this, girl? How did you know that my brother would betray me?" Camilla growled at the diminutive term.

I took a moment to answer, still looking absently at the wall. Without turning to meet Kroner's face, I murmured, "First of all, man, my name is Camilla Sekhmet." Kroner looked taken aback. Within me, Camilla barked out a surprised laugh.

He sputtered, "Fine, fine, Miss Sekhmet. How did you know?" Ah yes, a score. The modern approach had a few weapons of its own.

"Because," I said flatly, "my father sold him the bomb."

The room went silent but for the fire crackling in the background. Kroner sat back in his chair, making it creak under his weight.

"I see," he said finally. "It is apparent that Mr. Sekhmet did not expect us to be partners for long." Kroner paused again and leaned forward to tap one index finger firmly on the table between them. "Except ... how does this prove to me your skills with information? You would not have needed a network of spies for this tidbit." The old man looked amused and uncommonly relaxed for someone who'd just learned that his brother wanted him dead.

"Alexander . . ." Camilla's voice rose on my name, panicky.

Again, I hushed her. "I believe I mentioned," I began calmly, "that my father and I were not close. In fact, I was not privy to his machinations or motivations. He did not trust me. I had been keeping tabs on him via my own network. It stands as a testament to my abilities that I knew about this at all! In fact, I received first word of it from my South African contacts." That was true, in an odd, switch-backed kind of way. "My father was naturally secretive. Again, I was not close to him, and I have not even received official notice of his death from the authorities. And yet," I said, spreading my arms wide, "I knew enough to be here tonight and to set places for all who arrived. Though I notice," and here I grinned to show teeth, "that you are not as likely to drink wine from my hand as you were from his."

Looking down and away from my smile, Kroner chuckled. "It is true, Camilla Sekhmet, that I am familiar with family distance and the need to observe those family members from afar. That does not, however, help me trust your wine."

Behind Kroner, his edgy guards relaxed at the old man's easier demeanor. A knock sounded at the door—two fast, one slow, two fast—and the door swung open to admit the guard who'd left earlier. He gave the rest a quick hand signal; they had found no explosives in the car.

Camilla's nerves were beginning to twang my part of our shared nervous system. That could be disastrous. "Camilla. Please relax."

She snarled at me. "I'll relax when we get out of here. I'm not exactly trained for covert ops."

"You will be, soon enough." I winced internally at the thought. I hoped she hadn't caught the meaning of that.

Back to business. I pulled another business card from the inside of my long coat, and again flipped it across the table. This time, Kroner himself stopped its spinning to pick it up, but he kept his gaze on me.

I nodded at the card I'd thrown to Kroner. "I am much like my father in some respects, Herr Kroner. I believe in politeness. I do not demand payment up front for information, unlike my father, because I am quite capable of finding delinquents and stripping them bare myself. I do not make a living that way because I am a more than a common thief. However, I do find that ability a useful deterrent for some of my less polite clients." I motioned across the table. "That card has all of the information you will need to contact me should you decide to use my services."

Pushing my chair back, I stood gracefully. Kroner rose with me, tucking away the business card unstudied.

"You may expect to hear from me soon, Miss Sekhmet." He nodded, considerably more respectful than he had been when the group walked in the door a bare half hour ago. He turned to leave, three men preceding him, two following behind. When the door had shut behind them, I hung my head, suddenly exhausted.

Camilla immediately hovered over me, concerned. "Alexander? Hey, are you okay?"

I closed my eyes. It was definitely beginning to take hold, faster than I remembered.

Seating myself again, bolt upright, I shook my head. The posture comforted me. "I will be well, thank you, Camilla. I am merely overwhelmed by today's events. I have not needed to change so much of myself so quickly in a very long time." I sat staring at my fingers, small and delicate-seeming near the wine glass. With a sudden movement, I grasped the crystal and brought the wine to my lips, drinking it down like water. It didn't burn like whiskey, but it was better than nothing.

From thc outsidc, the barn owl touched my consciousness again. This time she had a report for me. I turned my thoughts its way to watch the rest of the evening's drama.

-ᴑᴑᴑ-

"Let go of me! Let go!"

Ian fought the men dragging him away from the cabin, his heels digging into the loose dirt. Something shoved Bill into Ian's back, and the forest whirled around them both as they fell down a small ravine. They stopped abruptly against the rough bole of a tree. Bits of bark and pine needles rained down into Ian's open mouth, choking and blinding him. Back at the top of the hill, one of the guards yelled something unintelligible. Bill shouted back, his voice raw and angry. He didn't get a reply. Ian was too busy trying to get his bearings to care.

"Ian!" Someone—Bill?—was shaking him, his teeth rattling from the force. Ian pushed and struggled, finally breaking free in a flurry of limbs. He scrambled to his feet and started crawling back up the slope toward the lit clearing.

Something clamped around Ian's ankle and locked tight. He jerked around and saw Bill's hand, holding him back.

"Bill," growled Ian, the voices clamoring approval of his bravery, "Bill, let go."

The grip on his ankle didn't lessen. Bill began pulling with increasing strength, dragging him down the slope. "Ian, if you go back there, my father's men will kill you. You can't go back!" Bill's voice was a high-pitched hiss, his eyes wide. He was frightened.

Ian slid down the last few inches to sit at the base of the pine tree, staring into Bill's pale face. Those dark eyes were like holes in the pasty skin, beads of dew glittering in his hair, on the bluish, cold lips.

"I want to get that smiling bastard just as much as you do, Ian. But," he hissed, "it is not possible that the woman sitting in there is the man who killed your father."

No!

He couldn't think that. Besides, it didn't matter if anyone else believed what he knew. He knew it, the voices knew it, but Bill didn't believe him. Ian searched Bill's face intently, a twitch shaking the corner of his vision. If Bill didn't believe him anymore, Bill was likely to get in the way. He might even take Ian back to the police.

"Ian? Did you hear me?"

The air was cold. Ian felt a shiver start at the base of his spine and travel up to make his shoulders shudder. Bill blinked, his grip loosening in confusion.

Now!

The word was a huge upsurge of encouragement, and he acted without a second thought. He flung himself down at Bill, hands raised with fingers crooked into claws. Bill took in a sharp breath of surprise, arms automatically moving to shield his face. All Ian saw was that lying mouth surrounded by corpse-pale skin.

They met at the foot of the slope, Ian charging forward, and Bill stepping backward. Those expensive-looking loafers slipped on pine needles, and Bill went down with a crash, his head slamming to a sudden stop on the base of the same tree Ian had hit earlier. There was a dull snap as Bill's head twisted sharply sideways, and the green eyes went empty.

Laying atop the dead man who'd gotten him out of prison only that evening, Ian reached out to stroke the short-cropped hair, the skin beneath it still warm. The voices swirled around him, now jubilant, now shocked, now laughing maniacally. Ian let them buzz about, barely distracted from the fascinating cat-tongue feel of Bill's short blond hair.

It was nearly an hour before Ian could tear himself away. By then, the forest had emptied of its visitors, and Bill was getting cold.

I withdrew from the owl's memories and scrubbed my face with my hands. This was not what I was made for, this skulking in shadows and speaking of lies. It had been centuries since I last missed my sister's guidance so keenly. She would have untangled this mess with ease. Regardless, I could not contact her. Even without the barrier of the years and words between us, I couldn't trust her. Especially not after my lawyer's reference to some "she" this morning.

"Alexander? What do we do now?"

I laid my hands flat on the glossy table, barely seeing what was in front of me. Camilla had an excellent question. What now? I should go home and begin building a network of customers for my new business. I would like to ignore the potential of Family intervention in my daily life. I desperately wanted to throw the whole day to the dogs and take myself off to the bloodiest battle being waged at the moment so I could lose myself in the slaughter.

"Alexander? Come on, talk to me!"

I inhaled sharply and got to my feet. "We're going back to your car. I have much to do."

Camilla's laugh tickled my throat. "Clearly."

I growled a wordless warning, and she went still. "What's going on? Are we in danger?"

"Is there any time that War does not involve danger?" The moment I thought the question, I wanted to call it back.

She didn't explode, however. "Listen. I don't like this stupid situation any more than you do." The expression she showed me was mild. "Do you want me to help or not?"

The cabin door swept closed behind us. "I'm not sure."

"Well, figure it out. You're not getting anything done now." I shook my head, but before I could reply, she barked out, "Wait, what's that?"

I followed her attention to the bottom of the ravine and caught a blip of light. The moon was reflected in a watch face.

I stopped, pine needles slippery under smooth-soled shoes. "That," I said, "is the body of Wilhelm Kroner."

Camilla absorbed this fact. "What a lovely man you do business with. He's a bigot, and he killed his son, too."

"No," I said, shaking my head, "young Mr. Dorsey did that deed."

Her internal aspect contracted in confusion. "What? I thought they were together. Where did Dorsey go?"

I bit my lip. "Something is riding him."

"Something like you?" Her voice was wary.

"Wha—no. I do not believe so." To be honest, I hadn't even considered it. "I rarely see other Family members. Ian Dorsey seemed unwell in his mind." I sighed and started the walk to Camilla's car. "I'm not even sure that he knew what he had done. He went back to his own vehicle several minutes ago."

"You really just don't see much that doesn't happen right in front of you, do you?"

Her tone irked me. "My sister is the tactician, not I."

"Which Greek god is she? Stratego?" Now she teased, like a younger sibling would.

I chuckled reluctantly. "She is not inherently Greek. Neither am I."

"Okay." Her voice was curious. "So what are you, then? Norse? Japanese?"

This could be the least contentious conversation I'd ever have with Camilla. "All of them and none of them. My siblings and I have places in those pantheons, but we are also another thing altogether."

"Siblings?"

I nodded. "Death, Plague, Conquest, and War." I tapped my sternum on the last word.

"Wait. That's almost the Four Horsemen of the Apocalypse. Except I don't remember Conquest."

"That misconception is popular, but Plague encompasses pestilence. And my sister Conquest has made a point of staying out of history."

"Holy shit."

"The world is more complicated than you were taught."

"Yeah." She shivered in the damp air. "So where's your horse, Horseman?"

"The Apocalypse is not here yet." Camilla's car was a dark shape off the road. I looked around and decided I would rather do this here than at home.

I pulled out a book of matches and struck one.

Camilla shook herself. "I swear to god, Al, if you smoke in my car . . ."

"Hush."

The flame grew into a column of soft, unwavering red. I waited, but not long. Hermes melted from the shadows, his suit now charcoal gray. He bowed, and the match flame bowed back.

Camilla felt hollow within me, like a fragile eggshell. "Who . . ."

"Hermes the Messenger," I said, hoping for a quick business transaction. "I need word—"

He stopped me with a raised hand. Opals flashed in the moonlight. "You have taken a new aspect."

I blew out the match, wishing it were in him to let something like that pass unremarked. "Indeed I have." I brushed the subject aside as though it were an insect. "I need word taken to Asag."

That caught his attention properly. Hermes' normally inscrutable face creased with revulsion. "War, you know I require double payment for that request."

I sighed, but was unsurprised. Asag, no matter what aspect he took on, was eternally repulsive. Currently, he occupied a small house on the outskirts of Boston, filling it with his hoard of rotting playthings and the pack of dogs that bedded in them.

"The message is also currency for you, I dare say." I resisted an urge to smooth the flyaway strands of Camilla's soft hair.

His eyes glittered gold. "The story behind your change of bodies would count toward it."

"Brother-cousin. I do not have time for this." Even had I the time, I'm not sure I would give it to him. The Messenger has taken my time and my coin in exchange for little in the past. His last visit gave me more questions and disquiet than answers.

"Perhaps you could make time. For Family's sake." Hermes folded his hands before him.

I kept my peace, staring at him. When he glanced down, I smiled. "I will tell it to you when we meet next. Surely, that is enough."

"Be sure you meet me again soon, then. You know I can't resist a good story."

"Very well." Close enough to a victory to calm even my sister. "Tell Asag that the weapons business is his to command, and that associates will be calling him. Tell him not to abuse this new position. Tell him I now go by Camilla Sekhmet, seller of tales." I looked away from Hermes' uncommon grin with a feeling like a knife slice. By our old rules, if I were human, that occupation would mark me as one of his. If I kept misstepping, blundering from complication to complication that clung to me like spider webs, I would be tied as tight as a captured fly by my own actions.

"I would not brave the Heavens for these lovely tidbits, but I will visit your second." He bowed, his expression returning to its usual quiet lines. Without further word, he disappeared back into the shadows.

Camilla had been silent during the entire encounter, an unexpected reprieve. Now, she spoke quietly, mental voice quivering with disbelief. "Hermes? Alexander, seriously? The Greek god, Hermes?"

I stared down at his fast-disappearing footprints. "Yes. He is my brother-cousin, Messenger to the gods."

"Jesus," she muttered, "how is this even real? I'm living a fairy tale." Her voice was a sick whisper.

Sensing that she was finally going into shock from today's events, I pulled out my flask of scotch and took a long, smoky pull from it. Camilla gasped at the exquisite taste and the flood of alcohol into her system. After she'd savored it, I unlocked her car and got in. She protested weakly.

"The drink is for you, Camilla. Don't worry, I will be driving."

Camilla was silent for a few minutes, internalizing knowledge and whiskey. When she spoke, her words slurred infinitesimally. "Why are the Greek gods hanging out on the East Coast of the US?"

I glanced up through the windshield at the stars in the clear sky. "They relocated here when your country was formed. The values that had created them were well represented by your founders, and the world was new." I grimaced. "The gods of America's native peoples did not appreciate the incursion, neither that of the whites nor of the Greeks."

"You can hardly blame them."

"I don't blame them. They fought well, both mortals and gods, and they fight still. Crow refuses to parley with us, and many of his people still worship the old gods. They don't need us yet."

"Yet." She thought that over. "You think they will?"

"I know it." Orion glittered before us, striding across the starry sky. "The People of the Book squeeze us all out in the end. Christianity, Judaism, Islam—they are all so strong. Even in the East, Buddhism takes the worship of those mortals not snared by Mohammed. The world's colors fade to black and white, and eventually it will be us against them. That will be true War, as I have not seen it since my beginning."

Camilla wanted to bury her face in her hands, and the feeling bled through the barrier between us. "Oh for fuck's sake. Can't you leave us out of your stupid war? You go beat on each other and leave humanity out of it!"

"We can't." Orion was slipping out of sight behind us. I focused again on the road. "We are all sworn to fight only through you mortals. When last we fought, many gods died. We destroyed many of the controls on the world's energy. Osiris was killed, and though Isis gathered his body together, she could not bring him back. Persephone died and her mother still mourns. Odin's ravens were slain, and many of the Valkyrie. We made a treaty, then. My brother agreed not to take another immortal if we stopped fighting each other directly."

"So you kill us instead." Such bitterness. Her thoughts were full of blood and sand.

"Do you think humanity would be peaceful without us?" I shook my head. "You are not that naïve. You would kill each other even if I had never existed."

She did not respond.

6

Stumbling Toward Battle

It was long past midnight before I returned to my home overlooking West Point. Had Camilla had control of her own limbs, she would have been swaying like a sailor just put in to port. The body we shared was exhausted and more than a little drunk. Rather than pull the alcohol from her system completely, I had let her drowse fitfully in the back of her mind as I drove.

When I pulled the Mustang into my garage, she shifted and yawned, gazing blearily at the bare gray concrete walls, my BMW parked next to us.

"What the hell, Alexander. Where are we?" mumbled Camilla as she fought dazedly to clear her vision.

I toyed with the notion of leaving her disoriented (and therefore without more difficult questions), but pushed back the unfair urge. I dismissed the alcohol from her blood and cleared her head. As she took her bearings, I closed the garage door with a gentle pulse of my will and moved toward the door of my home.

"Hey!" Camilla's voice was a hiss within me, hushed and alarmed. "What are you doing? Where are we?"

Reaching for the brass doorknob, I snapped, "We are at my home, Camilla. At least allow me the courtesy of sitting in my own chair before you begin your railing again."

My body stopped in mid-stride, right hand hanging in the air around the doorknob. Camilla had stopped me.

With a white-hot flare of outrage, I threw her to the back of her head and pinned her there, my mental image made of bone and blood-red fire. "Woman!" I roared, furious. "Do not think to catch me unawares. I will rend you limb from mental limb, should you attempt this again!" I considered doing it now, considered destroying her and watching as her ivory face withered before me.

Camilla shook, her mental fingers wrapped round my bony wrists. "What is wrong with you!" she gasped partly in fear, mostly in anger. "You don't know whether anyone's been here, whether your fucking 'associates' are here waiting for us to walk in on them! How did you ever survive at all when you're this careless?" Her eyes reflected my fire, throwing it back at me.

Grunting in disgust, I dropped her and withdrew as she glared, unrepentant. "I am not one of your cadets, Camilla. I know to the last termite and dust speck exactly what has passed the limits of my property. In fact," I growled, "nothing and no one has been closer to this house than the mailbox at the end of my drive, not since I left my land yesterday to find you." Swinging about, I pulled the door open with unaccustomed force and marched upstairs to my living room, lights flaring on as I passed.

"And I was supposed to know this . . . how? Dammit, you can't expect me to take orders from you without a peep!" I knew she could feel that point go home in me, and it was maddening.

The part of my mind occupied by Camilla's was silent as I stormed into the kitchen, throwing coat and cap behind me to fall to the floor. I could feel her eying my bottle of thirty-year-old Laphroaig and perversely turned from it to face the wide windows overlooking the Hudson.

She was still quiet minutes later, when the rolling of the dark waters had calmed me enough to speak with her. Taking a measured breath, I sat down on my flat beige sofa. The seat felt somewhat harder and larger than when I had last sat there. The change irked me. I did not enjoy giving up a position of power, and I found myself wondering whether I should have kept my strong, masculine body rather than taking hers.

It was far too late to reconsider. Sometimes, the jumps one makes on impulse are not easy to recover from.

Feeling a restrained tap on my consciousness, I turned to face Camilla again, my mask firmly back in place.

"Yes, Camilla?" I was proud of my restraint, even though the sight of her strained face had me thinking about blood again.

She seemed to see it. Her posture still ramrod straight, Camilla looked down and away. "Listen, I'm sorry. I just . . . ," she paused, then rushed out, "You really need to include me more. If you keep this up, I'll get scared and stupid at some point where it isn't harmless, and I'll get us both killed, and I can't live like that, Alexander, I just can't sit back here like some sort of expert manual to be called on when you need me!" Her face crinkling in frustration, she muttered,

"I don't even see what you see in me, anyway. You're doing just fine without me."

I studied her, thinking it likely that she had upended her career in much the same way she had upset me just now. I tipped my head back onto the back edge of the hard square sofa, considering. She had a good point, much as I was loathe to admit it. Perhaps I did not need her anymore. And the longer I waited to consume her, the more bleed-through I would experience from her personality. I had changed enough, could I even tolerate any more? I faced the thought with a surprising feeling of regret.

As I pondered, Camilla broke into my thoughts again. Her voice was tight, her words clipped and fast.

"How do you think your lawyer decided you were a demon?" The point of that was clear. She was trying to prove useful, as though the thought of me not needing her was uncomfortable. Perceptive of her.

I examined her question. How had Dorsey come to the conclusion that I was an evil entity? And why would such a man, prosaic to the core, leap to such a supernatural method of ridding the world of me? As I had known Dorsey, he was a man of the material world, given to ignoring oddities, interested only in the money his clients brought him. I had chosen him for those same reasons.

What had caused Dorsey to act in such an uncharacteristic fashion? He had seemed nearly mad with fear.

And why had I been avoiding this subject?

Camilla was fidgeting anxiously as I thought on this. I paused to glance back to her, my mind worrying at the bone she had tossed me.

"Camilla." My thought-voice was calm, and Camilla relaxed a fraction. "Why do you think Dorsey acted in such a way?"

She pounced on my question, a student desperate to return to the master's good graces. "I'm sure you have plenty of enemies. Weren't we just talking about gods fighting each other? Who hates you enough to mess with you this way?" She paused. "Maybe it has something to do with that kid, Ian. You said something was 'riding' him."

Oh hells. Her.

The world seemed to gasp with me as it all fell into place. I felt pole-axed. I had not seen her in so long, not since Troy.

Seeming to sense my utter shock, Camilla touched my mind again. "Alexander?"

I clenched my hands into fists. Would she dare . . . yes, she had proved it time and again.

"Alexander! What's wrong? What did I say?"

I exhaled the breath I had not noticed I was holding in. "My daimona," I whispered out loud. "Eris, if you have done this, you have much to answer for."

Camilla's mind buzzed as she searched her memory for that name. "Your what? Who's Eris? Your sister?"

I numbly shook my head and let it fall again to the back of the couch. My laugh was bitter.

Eris, the wild-eyed spirit of discord. Eris, the delighter in blood and strife. Eris, my former lover.

I needed more information.

I called the barn owl I had used in the forest to query it for signs of Eris that I must have missed. I had passed over an odd, one-sided conversation, which I reviewed now. Its contents woke me from my paralysis and deepened the hollowness in my chest.

The slight boy had not stayed long at the bottom of the ravine. He came back to kneel before the door of my cabin, hands to his ears. "Shut up, shut up! I can't even think now, shut up. . . ." The mumbled words rolled from his mouth, making little sense. He carried on both sides of a whispered conversation. No, more than that, it was as though a multitude of demons rode him, and rode him hard.

You've missed him!

. . . missed our chance . . .

He could be long gone. We must find him again!

You fool, Ian, you idiot!

. . . again, lost again . . .

Ian pushed his hands hard against his ears, though it was likely the voices were on the inside of his head as well.

Abruptly, one voice soared over the rest, a high-pitched, keening call. The familiar tones chilled me.

We can still find him, Ian. We can still bring him to his knees before us.

There was a moment of tense silence. Nearly weeping, Ian collapsed and whispered, "Thank you, oh thank you, thank you, thank you," his body shaking in reaction. "What do you want, anything, anything, just keep them quiet like that please, please, please—"

Quiet, Ian. You must be quiet, if we are to find the one who killed your father.

Tears still streamed down his cheeks, but the heaving sobs had stopped. He let his hands drop to his lap.

We will find him together, Ian.

Ian nodded helplessly. I knew the relief of acquiescing to her demands and felt for the poor, sick boy.

I could not save him. I could only hope I could save myself.

"You should go home, Olivia."

She felt her shoulders pulling up. "You know that's not going to happen."

Olivia's desk was filmed with dust and ash. Absently, she brushed residue from her notebook to clear the name "Bill Kroner." It looked like a curse word.

Sergeant Hernandez pulled a chair up next to her, shaking his head. "I know." He drummed his slim fingers on her desk and shot her a determined glance. "We're gonna catch this guy."

Olivia nodded, eyes unfocused. "I put out an APB on Kroner's registered car. Nothing yet. What's left of the squad is out looking."

Hernandez winced and rubbed his eyes. Ash coated his face, seamed with the trails of tears.

"I'm waiting for a confirmed lead." She rubbed at her own eyes and turned to meet his gaze. "The bastard is the son of an international arms dealer. I have no idea what someone like that would want with an arson suspect in upstate New York."

"I called the feds. Someone from the local office should be here soon to help coordinate."

"Good." Olivia's fingers tightened on the butt of her service piece. "Someone has to mind the store while I go out and get Kroner."

"Alexander?"

I had been obsessively cleaning my house for the last hour, polishing black-veined marble to a mirror gloss, working dust from tiny crevices, even getting down on hands and knees to scrub the black tile floors. My hands and shoulders ached.

My home was again a shining monument to sterility, all black and white and shades of gray. The only color flickered in the immaculate fireplace.

Camilla tried again, nudging me a little harder this time.

"Alexander. Wake up and talk to me." Her tone vibrated with anxiety and frustration.

Finally, I lowered my shield and allowed Camilla access to my thoughts again. I tossed the rag I'd been using toward the kitchen and made it vanish in mid-flight.

After a pause, Camilla ventured, "That's a handy trick you've got there. Could have used it on a couple of my cadets."

A grudging smile tugged at the corner of my mouth. That sentiment could have come directly from any number of sergeants, from pre-history to the present, as he cautiously nudged his commander into a softer mood.

When I didn't immediately reply, she tried again. "So . . . you had a fling with the spirit of discord, huh? Must have been a ride and a half." She cringed away from the crudity of her own question when I again didn't immediately respond, but somehow it suited. I did not want to dwell on the disgust I felt at the thought of Eris. I let Camilla's distraction work on me. I shook my head and seated myself on the sofa.

"For a very long time," I said aloud, just to hear a voice, "She was all the color in my world. Nothing could match her." My thoughts were distant, nostalgic, almost human in their regret. "She was my daimona, my companion and lover." I closed my eyes, to better remember her bright eyes, the sharp teeth and lush curves Eris had worn when with me.

"War and Discord fit together, like a hand on the hilt of a sword." I drew my own sword, fingers curling confidently around the ornate hilt. Camilla swallowed hard at the manifestation, but her concentration held. "For me, my position is a higher calling, a duty almost like that of a judge or executioner. One does not always enjoy the work, but it needs to be done."

She whispered, "What do you mean, a duty?"

I folded my hand tighter on my sword. "My siblings and I, the Four, are also the First. My brother was first of the First, formed when the first sentient being's death occurred. He called the rest of us into being to control other forces, before there were humans to give us our names, as he needed us. I followed closely behind him when the first beings came upon each other. Then came Plague at the head of the lesser armies of microbes, and finally Conflict brought strategy to men. After she came into being, the mortals could make their own gods."

I contemplated the bright sword I held level before me.

"Eris was one of them, formed by mortals' attempts to ransom chaos with worship. Unlike me, she found more than calling, more than purpose, in her position. She found rapture while provoking conflict, manipulating strife into being." The sword flickered red and blue on the blade though I held it perfectly still. "She was intoxicating, and drew me into conflict after conflict that she herself provoked."

I set my shoulders and sheathed the sword back into nothingness to stare at my empty hand. "I renounced her when the battle for the hand of Helen became inevitable."

Camilla caught the reference quickly, her realization shot through with disbelief. "Helen of Troy? What did Eris have to do with the Trojan War?"

It was so long ago that the story had been subsumed into legend. It was small wonder my soldier didn't know this small pebble that started an avalanche. I tried to explain, Camilla's physical voice in my control sounding low and fractured. "She was left off the guest list for some godling's wedding, and like a fool, I told her. She arrived uninvited and threw a golden apple at the feet of Paris of Troy. It was inscribed KALLISTI, or 'To the fairest.'" I ran fingertips across the surface of the couch next to me, recalling the softness of her skin.

"Three goddesses laid claim to it. Zeus refused to choose the winner himself. Instead, he demanded that the Trojan prince choose which of them had the best claim to 'the fairest.' Hera offered the young man power over the known world if Paris gave her the apple. Athena Nike promised wisdom and skill in battle. And Aphrodite dangled the heart of the most beautiful woman in the Greek world." I remembered the mortal's confusion, gods with flaming eyes on every side of him.

"So. Because he was a man who thought he could win the world for himself and learn the wisdom of the world by himself, he chose the woman." Shaking my head, I added, "Not even caring that the woman was already married." I felt a snarl ripple my lips. "He did not even know who she was. The spoiled brat did not care one whit."

"Did Eris care?" Camilla was absorbed, her lips parted in anticipation.

My chuckle turned into a choked laugh. "Of course she cared. It was exactly what she wanted, the perfect outcome. The most storied war since Lucifer's fall. She thought I would be so pleased."

Camilla's thoughts took on a strained feel. "Lucifer?"

I closed my wearying eyes and laid my forehead in the curve of my palm. "Camilla. Your stories about the Fall are almost as accurate as the ravings of a curbside preacher." I pinched the bridge of my nose between forefinger and thumb. "Just leave it be. We have much more pressing issues to deal with." The night was wearing thin, and I still had no clear plan.

Camilla counted to a quick ten and ten again. Of course she was interested, but we were wasting time we didn't have on these sidebars. I waited her out.

Eventually, she threw up thwarted metaphorical arms. "Fine. Let's just leave the most debated question humanity's ever come up with and focus on your little lover's quarrel."

By all that was or had been holy, she would not stop. "Be quiet, girl."

She stopped short, glaring. "What did you call me?"

"You heard me. I am bothered by your increasing need to question me." I had had enough, enough challenge, enough uncertainty. Enough.

Obviously, Camilla had not had nearly enough. "And you expect me to sit quietly on hold in the back of my own head, never thinking anything that you don't want me to think? I can't turn myself off, Alexander. I thought that's what you wanted me for, anyway!"

For a moment, I balanced on a knife-edge of pure rage. Then, without further thought, I surged to my feet and charged one of the large windows, bringing one fist up, drawn back behind my head. I felt Camilla panic as she scrambled to take control of her body. Truly mindless in the heat of the moment, I snatched her by the scruff of her mental neck and held her out of my way.

As she watched the first-person vision of herself fast closing in on a mirror image, I heard her fervently wish that she could at least close her eyes.

"You piss me off, royally."

Camilla was still sulking as I put my picture window back together. The last fragment floated back up to its place, and the cracks shimmered into clarity. Camilla shot me a thought colored in frustration and fear.

I fended it off and walked back into the kitchen, bracing myself on the edge of the ebony table. "You remind me far too much of Eris."

She recoiled as though I had slapped her. Perhaps she did not deserve such.

"I am not trying to tell you that you cause strife and take joy in it, Camilla. You do, however, seem to cause strife everywhere you go." The rage underlying my calm shell was wild and delicious. And familiar.

She stirred within me as though she felt it, too. She spat out words as though each one burned. "Then maybe I'm exactly what you need right now. You pompous know-it-all."

I couldn't tell whether she had any idea how that lit me like a bonfire. I wanted her to know it. To feel what I felt and fear it.

Hanging my head, breathing slowly, I licked my lips. "You may be more correct than you know, Camilla. Certainly more correct than I knew when I chose you." Reaching my right hand up to the tight bun at the nape of my neck, I pulled the pin and let Camilla's hair down. It was soft and smelled clean.

A finger of unease felt its way into my mind from Camilla. I shook my head and laughed at the feel of long loose hair on my face. I hadn't felt that for quite a long time. I sighed, the whimsical thought fading. Much that I had put behind me a long time ago was cropping up unexpectedly. I raked the mousy strands back from my face, thinking hard.

"Alexander."

I pushed myself up, looking over my shoulder at my dark reflection in the repaired window. Why did Eris do this to me? How did I become so much her puppet that her very name brought out the fire that I kept banked?

"Don't ask me to explain that. I may be a woman, but I don't get it any more than you do." Camilla shifted awkwardly within me. "People do crazy things when love is involved."

Trite advice from a twenty-six-year-old human woman. That was unlikely to be helpful.

"Let me tell you something about me. Trust, right?" She waited and continued when I refused to respond. "I've never had a lover. Not a boyfriend, or even a girlfriend. Nothing. I never wanted one." I focused more closely on her as the burning in my thoughts ebbed away. "I had friends, I had my parents. But the only people I've really cared for, on the level that people talk about lovers anyway, were my troopmates." She looked down, a blade of remorse cutting at her heart. "Those people had my back, and I had theirs. But they never understood why I wouldn't flirt, why I would never chase anyone. Why I always said no. And so they started talking. Something was wrong with me, and they knew it. And then I was promoted, and they were sure I'd turned them down in favor of someone else, someone who could get me a commission. It was never the same after that. Those people who I'd cared so much for just drifted away, and if I hadn't let them, it would have been worse."

I closed my eyes. "That is a hard road, Camilla. I am sorry for your loss."

She went on, her voice gaining strength. "Whatever you do, you can't think of Eris as your former lover, your former anything. There's too much history between you. You have to deal with her now, as she is now. Hey! Maybe," the thought struck her with an almost audible ping, "she'll be expecting you to be who she remembers. Maybe your goal of catching up with the world needs an accelerated timeline."

My hand still rooted in Camilla's hair, I paused. "I wish it were that easy, but I am not certain that I can tolerate a faster pace. You can see from my behavior tonight that I am near my breaking point." If I had a god to pray to, I would be on my knees in a second.

"What if you just took it directly from me? My memories, my opinions, my knowledge? It can't be more than a fraction of what you already have packed up in your head. Just do a quick copy and get me the fuck out of here." Camilla's subtext was so loud I couldn't even hear what she'd meant to say.

I put my wrist to my mouth as though to hide a cough and burst out laughing. The irony of her request was, of course, lost on her.

"Damn it, Alexander!" I seemed to have made her angry. How . . . appropriate.

I drew in a deep breath, sobering. "Camilla, you do not know what you're asking."

"What the hell does that mean?"

I knew my tone was becoming didactic but did not bother to rephrase. "I know how things work, much more deeply than you do. Than you ever could. My options in this situation are very limited: either I learn from you as a student learns from a master or I assimilate you."

That finger of unease poked out again, pushing me back. Camilla was beginning to catch on. Careless, I would ram the point home, a scene from long ago coloring my thoughts like a script.

I knew this was the end of our long sojourn together. So many armies crushed beneath his armies, so many conquests left behind. My sister had left him months ago, interested in nothing past the victorious looting and parades. She was never meant to rule, only conquer. I had even less reason to remain than she. I could feel other wars beyond his, itching necessities that had been eclipsed by Alexander's march to the sea.

It would not be long before my nature drove me to attend to them. Alexander knew it. The tent was thick with that knowledge and the stench of sickness.

"What are you saying, you son of a bitch?"

He moved in the dim light, and I knelt beside him, to be there when he woke. He would be my brother's dominion soon, and I felt an unaccustomed surge of possessiveness. I had barely had time to taste him, and soon he would be another's. It was unfair.

His eyes opened on what to him would seem utter darkness, his pupils blown nearly wide enough to swallow the dark iris. His throat ground out a dry bark of laughter devoid of humor, and I offered him a skin of wine. He batted it away feebly, growling low in response to the service.

Not quite gone then, not yet.

"Oh, so now you're finally shutting up? Great timing, asshole."

"Ares," he managed, breathing shallow, "this is a pitiful end for such as me."

I reached out to cup the clammy curve of his jaw. "It is," I agreed. What else could I say? He was right. The greatest living warrior deserved better.

A drop of body-warm sweat touched my hand. He pulled away, struggled free of his sickbed.

"Fix it, Ares." He shook with fever, hot as a dying torch. "Heal me! Save me from the death of an old man!"

"Why aren't you talking to me? Dammit, say something!"

I came smoothly to my feet, leather creaking. I did not put out a hand to steady him. "Brother of my heart, you know what I am better than most. I do not heal. I fight, I kill, I destroy." I paused. "And you are no longer in my purview. My brother will claim you soon, regardless of my own wishes. You know you have no more to conquer."

That crumbling laugh blew past me again. "Regardless of your wishes." Alexander stumbled, fell heavily against his rack of armor. He clutched it with a strength I'd thought beyond him. "Then you would keep me if you could?"

My heart thudded against my ribs. "I would," I grated out.

"What are you hiding? Answer me!"

His drawn face was lit with desperate energy, his gaze finding mine even in the darkness. "You wear the body of a mortal. I know you do." A cough rattled his body, wracking lungs that already wept blood. "Take me away from this! Take me. Take me with you, for I cannot stand to die without you."

"There is a price," I said.

"You would be consumed, Camilla, and there would be nothing left of you when I was done." My ire abating finally, a drop of worry stained my mood. If anything, this discussion was fueling Camilla's desire to escape even more, if not reviving it from cold embers. And there was even more I still held back from her. She was completely silent.

When I reached a thought toward her this time, Camilla pushed me back hard.

"Back off!" she yelled, "Get this straight. We're dealing with your business, we're dealing with Eris, and then you let me go." Her voice was iron-hard and brittle. "We are not friends. You don't get that part of me anymore. I'll do what you want, but you leave me the hell alone, otherwise!" Each word rattled with more intensity than the one before it.

The hollow in my chest grew. Had she caught my memory of Alexander? She could not possibly know that I did not have the power to hand her life back to her. And now I found that I did not have the heart to tell her. This was what humanity brought to the gods. A moral compass. Alexander had given me the same, before I finally decided to save myself from him.

With a terse nod, I acknowledged her, then swept her hair into a clumsy bunch and banded it tightly, the strands pulling on the scalp.

"Very well, Camilla," I said as lightly as I could manage. "We re-establish me on the world market, we deal with Eris, and no more will be asked of you." I hated that I felt so ambiguous about the necessary lie. I did not have the ability to let her go.

We both felt regret, I could tell. But neither of us would acknowledge it.

I am the goddess of discord.

Ian knew that couldn't be true. Discordia couldn't possibly be so soothing, so protective. He should know. Ian yawned hugely, still nervous and twitching. He couldn't focus. His mind kept wandering like a sleepwalker.

Ian, my child. We are nearly there, do you remember what to do?

He whispered an affirmative, though his head throbbed. Bill's car moved slowly. Ian couldn't seem to remember to keep the gas pedal down. The sky was beginning to get lighter. Was it morning already? Dark smears turning into gray smears. Did it even matter? Probably not.

Remember to let me speak when the time comes.

Ian nodded dumbly and set the drumbeat in his head pounding at a faster pace. He winced, the tic taking over the left side of his face for several seconds. Remember not to move your head, he berated himself.

"Eris," he muttered, "Can't you make my head stop hurting? Please?" Ian vaguely remembered asking this before, but maybe she'd just forgotten to fix it.

No, my pet. Then I would leave, and I know that you do not want that.

Moaning, Ian desperately wanted to put his head down on the steering wheel and weep out his frustration and pain. He knew he couldn't risk angering her. She might leave in a fit of pique, resigning him to a lifetime of chaos in his mind. The voices' quiet almost made the headache bearable.

Maybe she just wanted to test him, could that be it? Ian pushed the thought around as the dim landscape rolled by, deciding finally that that was the interpretation he would go with. Nothing else came to mind, anyway.

Whispering between his ears, Eris directed Ian to turn onto a long paved driveway, just where the trees finally broke to suburbia and were reduced to tailored, tamed copies of the forest. Though he was beginning to see interesting pinwheels and lightning-like stabs of light flit across his vision, Ian was able to maneuver the car between matched pines and then to a stop at the base of a large white house. Ian could vaguely see a slight figure pacing in front of a window. Eris seemed to tense at the sight.

Now, Ian.

Her voice was irate and anticipatory, impatient.

With the deed before him, Ian found himself hesitating. "Are you sure? Just open the door, and—"

He was cut off with a flash of agony that threw him out the door of the car and to the ground, retching. He didn't ask again.

By this point, the migraine pounding away at him was turning everything a delicate shade of pink. Or it could have been the dawn. Ian hardly could concentrate on more than putting one foot in front of the other. He wondered dully how Eris expected him to kill anything larger than a bug in his current state, but was careful not to let the thought pass his lips.

Finally, the steel double doors were before him, reflecting orange and gold from the sunrise over the river. Ian's own reflection was watery and indistinct in the brushed metal. Slowly, he put out both hands, as though to link fingers with the smudgy reflection of himself. The instant he touched the doors, they shuddered minutely and then flung themselves wide open, barely missing Ian on the outswing. Dizzy, he stepped over the threshold.

Somewhere in front of him, someone said, "Ian Dorsey?" The voices rose again, swirling in an almost visible tornado. No! he tried to scream, You took them away! Eris didn't answer.

When the whirlwind of voices settled, the pain was gone as though it had never been there. It was as though all nerve connection to his body had been severed. Ian tried to move and felt no response.

Instead, his lips moved seemingly of their own volition, speaking in a voice with the same horrible overtones he'd heard in the woman last night.

"Ares, my love. I have missed you."

7

Crossing Swords

"Detective!" Jackson hurried across the lawn currently serving as a temporary police station. He held a cell phone to his ear.

Olivia burst from her seat like a jack-in-the-box, heart pounding away her exhaustion. "Did we get a hit?"

"A lady called in a car parked across two driveways at a house on the east side of the academy. Plates match. Should we move in?"

"Hell no, Jackson. They hold off until I get there. Text me the address."

The S.W.A.T. van should have everything she needed. She checked her service weapon and extra clips as she grabbed her tactical vest. Shrugging into the bulky armor while running for her car, Olivia yelled back at the rest of the squad.

"We've got a line on him, guys! Get your asses in gear. We're after a cop killer!"

The crowd of fire personnel and EMTs parted before her, and her avid team followed.

When Ian Dorsey drove onto my land, I had prepared myself for a physical attack from the disturbed young man, in thrall to Eris. I had not been at all prepared for the voice of my erstwhile lover issuing from his lips. Eris had never deigned to ride a human. She'd always and eternally regarded the practice with disdain.

I staggered back in ridiculous disbelief, putting my left hand out behind me to catch at the wall. Within me, Camilla launched a flurry of questions that I paid no mind.

I should have been prepared for anything, after realizing that Eris could be behind all of the odd happenings of the past day. Dealing with George Dorsey had been like a bomb going off, my formerly quiet life turning into an instant battlefield. Unfortunately, regardless of any "should have," I certainly did not expect Eris to stoop to possession.

To my daimona, humans were no more than warring tribes of ants one led into entertaining conflicts before flooding the nests and finding new toys. They were not worthy of her interest, much less her habitation. And the treaty . . . hells, this broke the treaty. She had come bodily to my doorstep, and she could kill me here and now.

Dumbly, I wondered just how much Eris had changed over the millennia since our parting.

Camilla brought me to task with the mental equivalent of a stinging slap. Finally, the gears began to turn again, and I heard her.

"Start talking, Alexander! Get your bearings, start fighting back!" Her voice was strong, encouraging. "Don't stand there with your pants around your ankles, do something!"

Her metaphor was crude, but very apt. I straightened and stood away from the wall.

"I no longer go by that name, Eris," I said, forcing my breath to slow, "but as you like."

An ugly expression twisted Ian's borrowed face and vanished. "What then," she hissed, feral, "are you still fond of 'Alexander'? Your lover has been dead for centuries. I am not sure why you would keep his memory alive. But," she visibly restrained herself, smiling wickedly, "as you like."

My hands curled into fists, and Camilla slapped me again. "Don't let the bitch get to you, Alexander. If she has to win, she's gonna lose a few teeth first." I felt my face spread into an unexpected wide grin.

I spread my arms wide, palms up in a gesture of emptiness. Adrenaline brought aspen leaf tremors to my fingers. "Ages in the past. As, I had thought, were we. Our parting was very long ago, Eris, are you still wroth with me after so many years?" I leaned against the wall once more, a controlled move this time, as though unconcerned by her presence. "I would have expected you to put your talents to other uses and other loves by now."

Eris stalked forward, managing to make Ian's slight frame look menacing as she loomed close. "You, Ares, are a fool if you ever truly thought that I would forget a slight such as that one."

Camilla nudged me. "Stand up straight. Don't let her take your space like that." She paused to examine Eris' snarl. "How do you want to handle this?"

I shoved off the wall, bringing my face close to her borrowed form. Behind my smile, I thought to Camilla, "I want her disoriented, confused. She is a consummate manipulator, generally acting on a whim, with stellar instincts. How do you suggest I 'handle' her?"

Camilla bared her teeth, fully as wicked as Eris in her enjoyment of the situation. "I can handle that. Do exactly what I say. I doubt she'll be comfortable with the way I think."

Feeling my smile widen, I sent her a strong affirmative. This was what had drawn me to Camilla. Eris drew back a fraction, her eyes narrowing.

"Such an . . . odd . . . body for you to choose, Ares. Not like you at all. Not warlike, not even masculine." A hint of disdain, there.

I heard the faint sound of hissing in my head. "Punch her."

I was completely taken aback.

"Do it!" barked Camilla, her mind ablaze.

I subvocalized a curse at the thought of the dishonor I was about to do, but despite my reservations, I leaned forward and snapped the heel of one hand into Eris' borrowed jaw.

The reaction was surprisingly satisfying. Her eyes widened to show a ring of white around dark irises, and she staggered back, clutching her cheek.

Baring her teeth, Camilla laid out for me what I should say. Again I cursed, but again, I did as I was told.

"You are an idiot to judge by appearances these days, Eris. You may end up with more than a broken jaw if you keep that up." I resolutely kept my discomfort from my face. The tactic was working for the moment. "Now get out of my house." I was getting a grip on Camilla's plan of attack and added a few strikes of my own. "You have broken the treaty! Do you think my brother will take that lightly?"

"Do not hide behind your brother." Leaning forward, still cupping her jaw, Eris hissed, "What a difference I see in you, Ares. I am not sure I like it."

I sneered at her. "I do not care if you like it or not." Grabbing her by the elbow, I turned her around and began marching her toward the doors. "Just get out."

She yelped as I pushed her hand back up into her injured jaw, dragging her along in my current. "Ares! I need to speak with you! You cannot simply throw me out as you would a poor servant!"

The steel in the doors responded to my approach by swinging wide to let in the broadening day. "The hell I can't," I howled. Camilla had stopped feeding me lines, and I was as shocked as Eris by what I was saying, "I did not invite you in, and I don't want to talk to you. The rule of hospitality does not apply. It takes two to tango, Eris, and I am done dancing with you." I threw her past the threshold and sealed it against her with a concerted effort. As the supernatural barrier snapped into place, Eris threw herself against it, incensed.

"You cannot keep me out! You would not dare!" she shrieked, face flushed with anger and exertion.

"Watch me." The doors swung decisively closed; Eris barely made it out of their path before she was crushed between doors and supernatural barrier. The expression on her face was cold comfort to the extreme damage I'd just done to the spirit of the rules of hospitality.

Camilla whooped a war cry.

"You have lost all honor, Ares!" screamed Eris. She pounded the steel doors with her fists and screeched like a hawk.

Ian watched his fists slam against the door as though this were part of a strange dream. Paradoxically, he hadn't been this clear-headed or this confused in a very long time.

He'd lived with his voices for years, and while the volume had abated with treatment, they'd never actually gone away since then. But since he'd walked into that house—poof , nothing. Not even a whisper.

And I still can't move.

The previous day felt like a bizarre nightmare, as though he couldn't possibly have been arrested, broken out of jail, killed a man—Ian didn't really have any clear memories past that. He'd missed a whole day of classes, a day's worth of work on his dissertation, his father had died yesterday, and he couldn't move a finger to scratch his nose of his own volition.

He felt buried, like an animal in a box. That's probably how she thought of him.

And that's what he really couldn't believe, what sent the confusion to cloud his mind—Eris. He knew who—and what—she was, of course. Ian would be an unforgivably poor student if he didn't. He'd taught that myth to bored underclassmen for years, both the Greek and Roman versions, spinning the discussion of the golden apple into the Hesperides story and touching on Freya's golden apples of immortality. But it wasn't real. It wasn't.

It was hard to keep saying that to himself, though, with the spirit's thoughts raging banner-like across the surface of his mind.

Eris was angry, jealous, confused, even hurt. Her thoughts were like broad splashes of color, bright and vibrant and impossible to ignore.

She'd called that—woman, man, whatever—she'd called him Ares. Did she mean the god of war, the Greek god of War? It was impossible, but it was happening to him regardless.

Ian bemusedly shook himself. All of this speculation wasn't going to get him free of Eris. He had to try to get free. Mustering his courage, he reached desperately for control of his far-off body and failed. And failed. And failed. He wanted to weep in frustration.

His yells of frustration joined Eris' voice. Right now, he felt the most normal he had since he was a teenager, but he was still trapped in an insane situation and unable to do anything about it.

Eris threw bolt after bolt of energy at the house, each one sizzling against a barrier that flared red at the barrage. He could feel hurt and anger boiling in her, climbing at each failed attempt. Finally, she stopped, panting.

Ian tugged carefully at the hot female presence that had pushed him into the back of his own mind. It stirred, then turned on him, spitting like a cat.

"Little man, either stay in your corner or I will smash you to atoms!"

The face suddenly in his inner vision was feral, slit-pupiled, and unearthly beautiful. Ropes of long dark hair blew back from high cheekbones and skin that had the depth and color of amber silk. The full lips were twisted into a snarl over carnivore teeth.

He'd been expecting the angry threat, but the force of its actual presence threw him back. He felt as though he were being suffocated.

You've been through worse! he reminded himself. He had to get a better sense of what was happening to him, and that wasn't going to happen if he cowered and hid until it was all over. Ian clamped down on his fear and forced himself to look directly at his captor. "This isn't working! Whatever you're trying to do, it's not working. Let me help you. He can't be expecting that!" Now if she'll just take the bait . . .

She raised an eyebrow at him, her expression shifting to curious as quickly as if she'd button-pushed her way to the new emotion. "Ian Dorsey, you are much changed." She pursed her lips, eyes narrowing.

Ian forced himself to stand erect under her scrutiny, though his thoughts trembled. "Do I have you to thank for that, Discordia?" He hoped the anxiety coloring his voice wouldn't send her into another rage. After spending most of his lifetime trying to reason with the voices in his head, he knew how capricious and vindictive they could be, and he still wasn't sure whether Eris was real or a new manifestation of his schizophrenia. And the latter was a hell of a lot more likely.

The angular face seemed to consider his words and smiled. The expression was more aggressive than friendly. "I like that you recognize me. I do not like your lack of respect."

"Times change. Haven't you changed with them?" The words popped out almost without volition. This was exactly the sort of boldness the voices would have railed against yesterday. Now, it was heady to speak freely without chaos erupting in his mind. That trembling he felt in his thoughts—was it fear or excitement?

Eris's face lit up like a warning sign, and Ian cursed. Maybe just stupidity, he thought.

"I keep you alive because it amuses me, human, not because I need you." She glared at him and licked her lips with a small pointed tongue. "How could you possibly succeed where I fail?"

Bait taken. Ian steadied himself and ducked his head, trying to appear submissive. "My lady, brute force isn't working. Maybe we can attack from another angle, distract him with something else." This was like pleading with a bored, tenured professor; all he had to do was make her think of him as a submissive ally, and he'd have a chance at getting out of this alive.

Pursing her lips, she considered. "Do you have a suggestion, little advisor?"

Ian brutally quashed the smile he felt seeping into his thoughts. "I take my lead from you, my lady," he simpered, hoping she would be easy to flatter. "If we can encourage his business partner to distrust him, they would fight amongst each other. Then, he couldn't pay attention to you."

She cut him off, her eyes brightening. "And I could have him." She gave him a heavy-lidded smile. "Little pet, you may turn out to be useful after all."

Feigning bashfulness, he thought, I hope she means that. Or I may never get out of this.

"Did you see the look on his face when the door was closing? Goddamn, but that felt good."

I sat myself down carefully on my sofa, my hands shaking. Camilla's tactic had worked better than I had thought it had any chance to, but I had no idea what to do next. I could barely believe what I had done to Eris.

"Eris is female, Camilla." It was a foolish thing to say, but it was all I could come up with. Camilla snorted at me, confirming my own thought. I tried to direct her thoughts away from me. "What do you suggest we do now?"

Perhaps "crowing" was the wrong word. "Jubilant" seemed to fit better. "We fly by the seat of our pants, Al, and we watch her like a wolf following a sick deer."

At least that sounded halfway rational. "Alexander, please, Camilla. Let me keep at least a few of my preferences."

She paused, her mood seeming to dampen a bit. "Alexander," she said slowly, testing out the syllables. "Did you really sleep with Alexander the Great?" Her voice was incredulous, skeptical.

"The concept of the shield brother is fairly well documented, Camilla," I said stiffly. "Besides, you were rather scornful of Herzog's disapproval of his son's behavior, earlier."

Dismissing my statement with a thought, Camilla said, "And Alexander was a famous boy-lover anyway, I know. That's not what I meant."

I pressed one knuckle to my temple, where a headache was beginning to grow. "Then what were you saying?" I asked tiredly. I was not sure I was ready to handle this tangent.

"I'd figured that you were Alexander the Great."

This woman went from devastatingly exact to incompetent in a heartbeat. I began to laugh, rocking back in my seat, the nervous headache vanishing. "Oddly enough, you are almost right." Actually, my thought had maligned her. That had been an excellent guess, from someone whose education was so lacking.

Blinking, Camilla said flatly, "I don't get it."

Again, the memories played.

Alexander's voice broke, and I broke. I put out my hand to his cheek and steadied his weak limbs. "Alexander. You do not know what you ask." But oh, how I wanted to oblige him, here and now.

His skin had taken on a sickly pallor in the last few days, a pallor I knew well. Three of us had held him, each in turn. Soon he would pass from the penultimate domain to the last, and he would be gone for good. Now, though, his eyes burned brighter than Persian gold.

I let the explanation flow out of me, tired of avoiding the subject. "We conquered the known world together, he at the head of his armies and I at their heart." It was comforting to speak of, something I wouldn't have expected before all this.

"How can what I ask be worse than this death, this old man's trembling sickness?" he demanded, rage underlying his rasping voice. "You owe me!" I caught him as he slumped against me, his breath rasping and irregular.

"Alexander, I owe you nothing." Carefully, I guided the shuddering weight of him back to his cot.

"You owe me!" he raged. As if the anger fed him, he pushed me away with renewed strength. "I have given you war like no one ever has, or ever will. Take me into yourself, I know you can! You can save me. You can keep me with you, and the two of us can spend eternity together, waging war as we were always meant to!" The brief outburst left him panting, but still standing. I judged that he would not stand for long, though.

"When he reached his own limits, and I told him I would have to leave, he begged me to take him along, so he could live on at the hearts of other armies. So—" I hesitated, but the door had already been opened past retrieval, Camilla would never let this go.

I shook my head, undecided. "I can do something like to what you ask, Alexander," I said slowly, "but you would not be with me. You would become part of me." I surveyed his pain-ridden body and found an answering pain within myself. "We would neither of us be the same, ever again." I gestured at the body I wore as though he could see it. "I took this body when its true owner had passed into my brother's hands. It was a shell well-made to fit me. If I take you in the same manner, yes, part of you would live on. But you, the part of you that thinks and plans and loves and knows himself—that part would be gone. Only I will remain."

"I took his body and joined his mind to my own. I wore his flesh every day since, until yesterday." It was a sobering thought.

Alexander shook his head, laughing his choked laugh again. "Anything is better than this death, Ares. Anything."

Emotions warred within me, and I found pleasure even in that small conflict. Before I could think better of it, before reason caught me on tiger claws, I reached out and took his hand.

"So be it, then, brother of my heart."

"Holy shit, Alexander." She sounded awed.

I nodded. Indeed.

Then Camilla paused. I knew what she was thinking, even without invading her privacy, and it hurt. She was far too smart for her own peace of mind, and I was far too exhausted to avoid this conversation any longer.

"Alexander," she said slowly, precisely, "Are you planning on doing that to me?"

I sighed, closing my eyes. "I had hoped not to have this conversation." I paused, then murmured, "I am very sorry, Camilla."

I had to preserve myself, though it broke me to destroy her in the process.

Alexander's illness could not withstand my presence. I felt my siblings' amusement as they withdrew. The entire family would know soon enough, but I could not force myself to care.

For a few glorious weeks, I kept him safe behind the walls of my mind as I used his rejuvenated body to journey from one small war to another. The people of the other side of the world fascinated him. In the Aztecs, he found a people strange and bloodthirsty and proud, and his joy at them sent his restored laugh roaring through our shared mind.

Until the first day his anger took root in me, I hoped that we might escape the truly inevitable. When that red tide poured forth from me rather than him, when first I took the berserker's role and ripped a man limb from limb, and I stood in its aftermath soaked in gore, I fell sick to the ground. I knew I could not wait any longer.

Within us (within me), Alexander raged with an uncharacteristic chill, epithets and curses hissing from his imagined lips. I gritted my teeth and allowed it. Perhaps I deserved it. Perhaps I merely wanted something to remember him by.

In the space of a breath, she flew into a blinding rage.

"You bastard. You . . . you rapist! This is worse than rape, you're taking my soul away without even asking me what I want, you weren't even going to tell me, you son of a bitch! What the fuck is wrong with you?" She was on fire, breathless with her anger. "You think of yourself as such an honorable warrior. How the hell is that honorable?"

When he finally fell silent, I spoke. "I told you. I did not want this. The loss of self is harder to accept when it stares you in the face, but it is no less impossible." I shook my head, biting back at the wash of rage that was becoming more and more familiar. "If I do not take you now, I will become more and more like you until you are completely absorbed. And I wish to keep more of myself than that process allows."

I stopped her flow of words with a thought, though I knew it would make her even more angry.

"I need someone, Camilla, a young, strong body with a mind suited for my tasks. I gave up Alexander's flesh, and I need a new home." I paused, then added quietly, "I wish it didn't have to be you."

I could no longer hear her voice, but her emotions were still projecting strongly: anger, fear, betrayal. The last goaded me into an explanation, though I knew she wouldn't listen.

He spat derisively and turned his back on my image in our mind. The red dog of my new temper bit me, and without a further word, I took him into my hands and inhaled him and crushed him and felt him dissolve within me, salt in soup, gone.

"Once I let go of Alexander's body yesterday, it went to dust the way it should have centuries before." This was harder than my confession to Alexander. Guilt swamped me in a black wave. The part of me that was once Alexander insisted on adding, "It will not hurt, Camilla. And you will live forever."

Alone with my thoughts again, I balled my fists and roared. A tree beside me blasted to tinders.

Camilla flung herself away from me and did not respond.

"There's got to be something I can do to get out of this."

Camilla paced a worn track in the back of her mind, cursing to herself. She'd been turning over and discarding plan after plan for a good hour now and was no closer to an answer than she had been.

Alexander (that name was starting to give her the creeps) had tried to get her to talk after dropping this morning's bomb. She hadn't given him so much as a peep, and he'd eventually left her alone. He'd gotten more and more irate with each moment she ignored him, and while he was still just below his boiling point, but not for much longer. She absolutely needed to come up with a way to trick him into letting her out, as soon as possible.

As if anything I do is going to keep a supernatural being off my back, she admitted to herself, worrying about the problem. She needed to become more trouble than she was worth, make herself a pill he didn't want to swallow. Not very fucking likely, unfortunately. She hadn't felt this helpless in a really long time.

Strategy, then. The bastard clearly didn't think much past the next few minutes. It was why he said he needed her—to clean up a mess he'd made and didn't know how to fix. If she could just catch him off guard, distract him long enough for her to get control, or at least botch his goddamn plan.

He took her for a weak woman, as though those words were welded together. There was a crack in that, something she could use.

Huh. It reminded her a bit of her last rugby game in high school, actually.

"Jim, you take the ball and either run it or get fouled. Don't let them have the damn thing this time."

"Chrissake, Cam! It's not like I meant to turn over the ball." Jim's broad, crook-nosed face was bright red.

She cut him off with a sharp gesture. "I don't care what you mean to do, I care what you do. Do it right this time or the finals are over, thanks to you, and you know it!" Cam stared him down until his eyes flicked away.

"Got it, captain." The burly teenager took a deep breath and shook out his hands, suddenly grinning. "East doesn't know what they're in for!"

Cam blew a strand of hair out of her eyes. "What does that mean?" Game four of the finals, and they had to win this one or they were out, and Jim was busy puffing his chest out.

His grin grew sharp and vicious. "Their forward told me girls can't play rugby. That's why I fouled the bastard."

Her eyes narrowed, and her heart sped up as though something were squeezing it tight. "Excuse me?"

Jim shrugged, too off-the-cuff to be real. "They can't talk about my captain that way and get away scot free."

Cam's vision narrowed to include only the other team, lumped together in an amorphous blob at the far end of the field.

"Fine," she said, and barely heard Jim's cheer. "Let's show them I'm no stupid girl."

I'm not helpless, she insisted to herself. He needs me for something, or I would have been lunch a long time ago. And anytime you've got something they need, you've got leverage.

So. What did Alexander need from her that he couldn't get by absorbing her? Her memories and experiences he could have in an instant, her body, too. She shuddered. The thought chilled her blood and made her want to crawl out of her skin.

Given all that, given that he had her memories, her body—what was left? What did he want?

The only thing he wouldn't have was her. Her thoughts, her way of thinking. Something in her chest loosened. That, she realized, has got to be it. It's not as if he could possibly be sentimental about me.

He could have taken anyone, literally. Anyone living today would think differently from the way Alexander thought, but he obviously needed a soldier. Any soldier would have the same sorts of experiences and memories that she did, but would probably be more conservative. Camilla was a modern fighter, and her tactics had to be outside anything Alexander would have considered.

He was keeping her alive because he needed a partner. An equal partner.

Suddenly, she wanted to laugh. The bastard can't eat me, she marveled, then sobered and thought, at least, not for now.

And that had better give her time to figure out her next step.

Camilla wasn't going to let this stuffy sonovabitch kill her, not without stealing everything of his she could lay hands on. Even if the only way to win was to make him lose.

"Let us tally our arsenal."

Now back in Bill's car, Eris opened the glove compartment and pulled out papers—repair history, car insurance, maps. Throwing them around the car with complete disregard, she dug down and pulled out two objects Ian recognized instantly: a cell phone and a gun. He felt her smile. "Pet," she said aloud, "these will be our tools." She hefted the gun, popped out the magazine and nodded to see it full. Pushing it back in with a snap, she laid the gun on the passenger seat and considered the phone.

Ian wavered. He'd never been comfortable around guns, even toys. And this was definitely no toy. It was huge and heavy, and Eris seemed to know exactly what to do with it.

Eris flipped the phone open and looked steadily at the display. "For this, pet, I will require your help."

Inwardly, he leaped at her words. Constraining himself, he nodded. "Anything my lady asks will be done."

Her eyes narrowed, and he cursed. That may have been laying it on too thick, he muttered to himself. Be careful. He smiled as ingratiatingly as he could.

Seeming to dismiss his crawling tone for the time being, she said, "Tell me how to use this." She waved the phone across his field of vision.

"Uh . . . is it on?" How do you explain a mobile to a goddess?

She rolled her eyes in an extravagant gesture. "This will take too much time. Time I would rather spend on Ares." She paused, and something fluttered in her mind that Ian didn't catch.

"I will allow you access to this body so you may use this . . . thing." Her nose wrinkled in distaste. "But do only as I tell you. If you attempt to take advantage of me, you will never see the light of day again." She grinned broadly, showing him her pointed teeth.

Ian hunched in on himself, feeling like a rabbit negotiating with a cat. "Of course, my lady, I would deserve no less." He let her see the fear she'd inspired, and the grin relaxed into something more satisfied.

"Good," she purred. "Now, I want you to contact Ares' associate, the one we met last night. I will take it from there. Once this ball is rolling, it will not stop until I have what I want."

With no sense of transition, Ian was suddenly back in the driver's seat again. He could feel the phone clenched in his fingers and the rise and fall of his chest as he breathed.

Hang on, remember that this is just the first step. She doesn't trust you yet. Frightening how much that sounded like one of the voices.

He swallowed hard and forced his shaking fingers to flip through the saved numbers on the phone. He found the one he wanted almost immediately, labeled "Father – US." Hoping the quaver in his hands wouldn't creep into his voice, he pushed SEND and held the cell to one ear.

It rang once, twice. "Come on, pick up," he muttered, his free hand fisting in his lap. Finally, there was a click.

The voice was dark on the other end. "Wilhelm. This is the last time I answer your call. Now be quick."

Ian tried to draw breath to respond, but found words already prepared and spoken. "This is not your son, Mr. Kroner. But I do have information about him that you will want to hear." The words popped out before he had a moment to think. It seemed that Eris was still in control of his voice.

Kroner paused and answered carefully. "Talk, then."

Supremely confident, Eris answered, "Wilhelm has thrown in his lot with your old arms dealer."

"Impossible," he scorned, "Sekhmet is dead." His voice held a faint note of unease.

"He and his daughter would be quite pleased to hear you say that."

The line was quiet for a few moments. When Kroner spoke again, he was expressionless. "Why should I believe you?"

Eris chuckled. "Can you afford not to? Call the daughter and ask her for information you already have. If she stalls you, or lies to you, it may give you your answer."

Following a wordless command from Eris, Ian flipped the phone shut. She radiated warm approval, and took back the reins of his body. He watched carefully, feeling the way she settled herself just so in the command center of his brain. It was as though she issued commands and set up roadblocks, rather than pulling strings. Most things going on in his body were still running themselves: heart and lungs, senses recording and running messages directly to their new captain. She seemed tense and precarious in her grip, and Ian wondered if he had the guts to try to dislodge her. He could certainly see how she'd wormed her way in, now that he had watched it.

Now that I know how she does that, he thought grimly, she won't be able to keep me from doing it. Hopefully.

"Goddammit." Olivia shielded her eyes from the midday sun and scowled.

By the time the S.W.A.T. vehicles pulled up to the enormous house overlooking West Point, the red sedan Olivia was hoping for was gone. She spat bitter curses and pulled away from the other officers before they could offer comfort and encouragement.

We can find them, she thought viciously. They've got to be here somewhere.

She handed her rifle to the closest officer, ripped off her tactical vest and helmet, and jumped out of the black municipal van.

"Liv, where are you going? We've got to search . . ."

Don't call me Liv. Olivia stopped him with an upraised hand. "I'm going up to the house, see if the occupants saw anything. Lee, Cicero, you're with me." She abruptly turned back, and the objecting officer flinched.

"If you find them, hold them and call me immediately." Resuming her march to the front doors, Olivia couldn't help but marvel at the size of the house in front of her. It was practically a mansion made of glass and steel and concrete, an odd bunker of a protrusion in the predominantly Edwardian neighborhood.

Somebody thinks he's important, she thought.

"Camilla. I have been very patient." And unusually gentle.

As I expected, she did not respond. Before I could try again, the doorbell rang.

Both of us tensed. I put down my scotch and walked to my door. My hand itched for the hilt of my sword.

Instead, I pushed the double doors open and found the police on my doorstep. I had not noticed the intrusion, and I felt a deep pang of fear. My carefully ordered world was falling apart. The police and I blinked at each other.

Camilla radiated surprise and recognition. She knew one of them.

The dark woman heading the group opened her mouth to speak and shut it without a word, confused. A name filtered up from Camilla's thoughts.

"Olivia?" I asked, uncertain.

"Camilla," she responded, regaining her balance. "I thought you lived on campus."

Oh hells. Had someone noticed Camilla's absence?

"I . . . not always," I ventured, watching the woman's face. It was lined with exhaustion and anger.

Olivia shook herself. "Whatever. I don't care right now. I need to know if you saw anyone on this property recently. They were reported to have parked a red sedan in this driveway forty-five minutes ago. They are both mid-twenties, slim, white, named Bill Kroner and Ian Dorsey."

My jaw dropped. How—what—could she possibly know about Dorsey?

Her face tightened at my expression. "I'm going to need to come in and speak with you, Cam."

No. Absolutely not. "I can't do that. I don't even own this place." A thought struck me. "I've been waiting here for the owner all morning, and I can't let people in without his permission."

Within me, Camilla snorted derisively.

Olivia's shoulders dropped, and she passed a hand over her face. "That would be because he's probably dead, Cam."

Playing my part as well as I could, I clutched the doorframe. "Dead?"

"We'll explain it later. Right now, I need information on Ian Dorsey and Wilhelm Kroner." Olivia's lips curled as she spoke the names. I wondered what Eris had done.

"Ian Dorsey? Why do you want that kid?" I asked, cagey. "He stopped by earlier for about five minutes and left when I wouldn't let him in."

Olivia latched on to the admission. "Just Dorsey? He was alone?"

I shrugged. "Yes, just him."

"Did you see where he went?"

I shook my head. "No. What did he do?"

Olivia's eyes were slitted and fiery. "He burned his father's office to the ground, then broke out of custody after Kroner murdered my partner."

That sounded about right.

I put a hand to my chest, hoping to look shocked. "Oh my god. I had no idea! I'm so sorry, Olivia."

Hurt flickered through Olivia's eyes, to be followed by disgusted rejection. "You know, so am I. I don't know what you're doing here, Cam, and I really don't want to know." Camilla bit her lip. "Just—I'll call you later if I need to talk to you about this. Goodbye."

Olivia turned smartly and strode off, her puzzled entourage in tow.

Camilla's voice was bitter. "One more thing you've ruined for me, Alexander. That woman was my friend."

Baffled and annoyed by the exchange, I pulled my doors shut. "Does it matter, Camilla? Really?"

"It would be nice if someone missed me." And with that, she withdrew again.

An hour later, I had switched from scotch to a dark burgundy the color of blood, and the bottle was half empty before I sensed her movement.

Finally, Camilla unfolded herself from her back corner and presented herself, expressionless. I looked her over with an equal wariness, seating myself facing the window I had broken last night.

After it became clear she would not speak first, I granted her the point. "Are you well, Camilla?"

I meant to be solicitous, but the twitch that briefly flitted across her face was not reassuring. "I'm as well as you'd expect, Ares."

Ares. That did not bode well.

"Camilla," I tried again, "I know that this is unfair. I know you deserve better, are better than a costume for me to assume. I simply have no options."

She shook her head. "You always have options. You just have to be willing to take them." Her eyes were burning.

Sitting deeper into the hard sofa, I surveyed my young prisoner. Her mental shield had gone from translucent to opaque in the course of an hour. I could not read her at all, which was more than I had expected of a mortal. I wondered what she possibly thought she could do.

Camilla shrugged, the impression of movement as inscrutable as her perfectly controlled expression. "Obviously, I've been thinking. It seems like I have no choice here. You hold all the cards." She was matter-of-fact, distant. I gave her a wary nod. She was certainly leading up to something, but in a fashion I had not expected. Polite, almost mannered.

Calmly, Camilla settled her mental image into a lotus position, legs crossed, feet tucked gently atop her thighs. She'd clothed herself in a loose white gi, her black belt knotted carefully. I was struck with the realization that I hadn't noticed the change and felt a twinge of alarm. Another chink in my armor.

"You have unimaginable years of hard experience on me, especially in this particular arena," she went on, gesturing at the blackness of her mind surrounding us. "And I have little chance of ousting you from my body and even less chance of escape." Camilla glared bitterly. "Were it even possible, I have no idea where that would leave me."

I felt tension creeping into my borrowed shoulders. "Camilla, this tone you have adopted is far from your usual manner of speech." The inquisitive, casually crass soldier I had met yesterday could now be easily mistaken for the heroine in an Edwardian romance. What was she doing, and why? She was right on all counts. Why then would she admit it so baldly?

Expressionless, the young woman looked down in what was obviously a calculated display of subservience, even turning her head to one side to expose the elegant lines of her neck. "Sir," she said in an amused tone, "I adopted a common manner of speech we both understand. You see, I want no further misunderstandings, no more critical information held back." Her eyes were still cast down in an attitude I had to admit was appealing. "In plain terms, I submit, sir. I surrender."

I leaned back into the unyielding planes of my couch, considering the relaxed image of womanly subservience before me. I did not trust it, not after spending the better part of a day with Camilla Sykes as she truly was. My concern was increased a hundredfold by this obvious subterfuge. Now I had no idea of her motives, her thoughts, her opinions.

I was certain of one thing. Camilla knew I could see that she had brought our battle into a new arena, was in fact thumbing her nose at me. I would need to scrutinize everything she said from now on. She had just announced that she had removed herself from my list of assets. It was a dare, a play at forcing a compromise—one I absolutely could not afford. Perhaps I should take a page from Camilla's own book in response.

"Bullshit, Camilla." The words were so foul in my mouth, but they finally elicited an involuntary reaction. She flinched. Good. I went on. "If that is how you want to play this game, I cannot force you to stop." Her lips curled up in a smug smile, and I smiled back fiercely. "Not without assimilating you now." Her smile flickered. "But remember that, as you say, I have ages of experience on you. I know what you believe you are doing, and I have won before with far less on my side."

The muscles in her jaw bunched. Her eyes cold, she fired back, "Then I call your bluff, old man. Chew me up and have done with it." Leaning forward, she spat, "Just remember who got Eris out of your house, before you do."

I felt a great urge to fling my wine glass at the window before me. I set it down with slow control and stood. At that moment, my phone rang.

We both jumped at the shrill, unexpected sound. Normally I was annoyed by the interruptions put upon me by this society's technology, but today I was glad of the distraction. I turned and went into the kitchen.

Camilla rolled her eyes at me. "Goddamn it, Al, just let it roll to voice mail."

Clipping each word precisely, I said, "I do not have voice mail, Camilla." I picked up the handset and brought it to my ear. "Sekhmet."

The voice on the other end, while not entirely unexpected, was certainly a complication. Hertzog Kroner.

"I require some information, Miss Sekhmet."

8

Betrayal

"What are you doing?"

War sat himself at an enormous desk of glowing golden wood. Camilla was certain its cost was equally enormous.

"Do you actually have access to that information?" He couldn't possibly, troop movements in Afghanistan were seriously classified.

Without answering, Alexander pulled a manila folder of documents from the depths of a file cabinet and opened it. He flipped it to a map and pulled it out to unfold it. The thick brown paper covered the entire desktop.

The surface was a map of Earth, multitudes of small red dots clustered in random areas across every continent. Alexander tapped the irregular shape of Afghanistan and drew a circle around it with his index finger. The map fluttered, pixelated, and resolved to a full-map view of the country.

Damn. Nothing new under the sun.

A few more iterations of the same process led to a close view of an area north of Kabul. Troop numbers, alliances, everything spelled out like a street map. And it was moving.

Blocks labeled as US infantry were creeping east, toward a concentration of Taliban troops in the foothills. A small city was marked nearby, labeled as Tagab. Alexander reached for a pen.

No! She couldn't let this happen. She was a US Army soldier, and this was her sworn duty. Protecting this information was worth a risk.

Carefully, oh so slowly, Camilla reached, not for control of her body or Alexander's mind, but for the name of the city that Alexander had just read. It was right there, on the skin of his thoughts, only to be remembered for the next few moments.

Any other town, she thought, any name is better than the real one.

There was another city about two miles away. Doran.

Camilla filled her thoughts with that word, humming it to herself, aiming at that city poised at the top of Alexander's thoughts.

His pen scratched troop numbers and speed and supply lines on the notepad in quick shorthand. He began to describe the terrain.

Doran. Doran. Doran.

The pen quivered, and he wrote Doran.

Camilla gasped in relief. With a gargantuan effort, she folded up the reaction as small as possible and watched Alexander put the map away.

Please let that be enough.

"Eno, dio, tria, tessera . . ." I counted quietly in Greek as I worked.

My script was smooth as ever, though Camilla's smaller hands warped it enough to make it unfamiliar. Numbers, dates, troop movements, and rough maps filled several sheets of thick paper. The ballpoint pen I'd forced myself to use felt flimsy and light.

"Pende, eksi, efta, okhto . . ."

Camilla was disturbingly quiet and had been so since Kroner's phone call. The cause was clear: the information I'd been writing down for the past hour. Kroner had asked for data on troop movements in the Middle East, including those of the US military. I knew she vehemently disapproved.

"Enea, deka . . ."

Finally, I sighed and put down my pen.

"Your silence will not keep me from this task, Camilla." I cracked knuckles tight from the past hour. "I value honor highly, but I have a far more important goal than patriotism."

Her disagreement was a sharp head bob in our shared space. "No way. I'm not participating in this." Prickly and cold, her presence paced the bars of her cage. "You should know better than anyone."

Restraining an urge to pick up the pen and thrust it through a wall, I instead snapped Kroner's information into a neat stack and slipped it into an envelope.

"Why do you even care?" she burst out, giving me her full attention. "If I can't stop you, what does it matter what I say, or do, or think?"

I shook my head, swallowing down a surge of unexpected panic. She was right. I had no reason at all to concern myself with her consent or lack of it.

Unless the internal walls were beginning to crumble. No! No, it was far too early for that. Perhaps I merely enjoyed her presence, missed the commentary and company of the past day.

"Alexander?"

I came back to myself to realize I'd stopped cold, envelope halfway to my breast pocket. I completed the motion and rose to my feet. Camilla's worn Ford key in my hand was hard and familiar. More familiar than it should be. My hand clenched tight.

"What the hell, Alexander!"

I shook myself, wrapping my body's urge to tremble in my steel will. This entire charade had gone far enough. I plucked the phone from its cradle, dialed a well-known number. The wait was short.

"Kroner."

The handset was cool against my skin. "I have your information. When can you meet?"

The line crackled to itself for a moment. "First, one question."

"Herr Kroner," I said, the roll of my eyes delicate but obvious in my tone, "I will happily verify my information by telling you the tidbit you already know."

"Ha!" Was that Kroner's or Camilla's rough laugh? No, Camilla was a tight ball inside me, mute and shaming.

Kroner's voice thawed appreciably. "Yes please, Ms. Sekhmet. Just the name of the current town will suffice."

"The name is Doran."

"You're certain?" Kroner insisted. His voice was light.

"The information comes directly from the US military. My contacts are good." Alexander did a very good impression of a bored, irritated expert when he wanted to.

Kroner paused, then, businesslike, said, "Very well. Meet me at the usual place for payment. In one hour." The phone line went dead.

Alexander's brow furrowed. Setting the phone down with a gentle click, he mused, "That is somewhat unlike Hertzog. He is usually much more polite." He sat staring at the phone, apparently lost in thought.

Feeling a chill run up her spine, Camilla interrupted hastily. "Maybe he just doesn't trust the new character yet, so the treatment is different. I don't know. Let's just get this over with."

Unhurriedly, Alexander stood and made his way back toward her car. "You may be right, Camilla. But to be cautious," and here he smiled cruelly, "I'll be prepared for trouble."

He paused, looking down. "I am sorry, Camilla. I appreciate the difficulty of your position. I wish things could be different."

Fighting down the surge of guilt, she sent him a curt nod and hurried him out the door.

The drive back to my cabin in Storm King Park was uneventful and very quiet. Late afternoon shadows lay long and spindly across the highway. I knew it would take me about forty-five minutes to get there, potentially time enough for Hertzog to arrive there before me. I would have to be very careful.

Camilla was distant, though I could hardly blame her. The withdrawal following my admission of her coming fate was unavoidable, but I found I missed her running commentary, as crass and frustrating as it could be. I had not shared such intimacy since, well, since Alexander.

I shook off the nostalgia as I approached the gates to the park. I would mourn Camilla when she was gone. Now, I did not have the luxury of time.

The woods were calm as I drove down the gravel road. I stretched out my senses to scout the terrain, speaking to the hawks circling above, the carrion crows in the trees.

And by such simple actions are empires saved.

My cabin was surrounded, the woods near it peppered with men carrying sniper rifles. Hertzog himself had broken down my steel door and sat waiting at my table, in my seat, a bottle of my wine before him. He held a glass in one hand and a pistol in the other. Behind him stood Ian Dorsey, the shadow of Eris twisting his features.

Chagrined, I reflexively let off on the gas pedal and the Mustang slowed. Within me, Camilla snapped into battle-ready focus.

"Alexander? What's wrong?" She was alert, anxiously attempting to see what I had seen.

I brought the Mustang back up to speed. As I was within their perimeter now, I did not want to reveal what I had sensed. To Camilla, I said grimly, "This is an ambush."

"What?" She sounded crestfallen rather than surprised, and I spared some attention to study her. Her mental image was wan. "Oh shit. Goddammit."

At that point, I knew what she had done and would have taken her immediately in my rage if not for the coming conflict. "You tricked me, Camilla." My fingers were leaving dents in the steering wheel that would still be there when I let go.

"Yes." She was panicked, obviously aware that this meant danger for her as well. "How did he know? Alexander, I just—I couldn't—"

I silenced her with an angry gesture. I knew why she had led me astray, and while I sympathized, she had put us both in a precarious position. And how had she managed it? I should have been able to sense the lie at the moment of its inception. The question nagged at me even as I put it aside. Could she truly be seeping so far into me so quickly?

I could not know for certain what was coming, but I could not allow her to distract me. I would deal with her betrayal later. For this, I would not need her advice. Dorsey's betrayal was familiar, barring Eris' impressive presence and power. If I could remove her from the scene quickly, I would be left with a scenario I had dealt with many times over.

Fortune willing, I would be able to do so again.

I pulled the car to a stop close to Hertzog's BMW, pausing for a moment as the engine pinged in the quiet. I could see no one in the clear-cut circle of my land, but the hawk circling above whispered the locations of seventeen men surrounding the cabin, sniper rifles aimed at me. I shook my head, a snarl pulling at my lips. The immediate situation was hardly dire. I could handle any amount of damage to my person as long as I was sufficiently prepared for it. While Eris herself could do me serious harm, I could not conceive of even her willingness to break the treaty that openly. The necessity of dealing with the mortals, however, irked me. My safe, secure world had tumbled into chaos, and that made me angry. A recriminating part of me whispered that I had begun this series of events myself, and I quashed the thought savagely.

Controlling my movements, I exited the car and strode confidently to the door of my cabin. Sunlight glinted off rifle sights as they followed me.

"Sorry, lieutenant. There's just nothing here."

Olivia watched Cicero walk back to his team and growled under her breath. There was nothing to find here. Kroner and Dorsey had apparently driven here, were denied entry to the house, and had driven away. To top it off, Camilla had left about an hour ago. This day couldn't stop punching her in the gut.

"Dammit," Olivia hissed to herself. She ran one hand over her close-cropped hair, staring at nothing.

"Detective?"

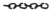

Olivia jumped and then scowled at the tech at her shoulder. "WHAT."

The tech (God, she knew the woman's name, she could find it if the buzzing in her head would just quiet down) looked at her sidelong for a moment. She said cautiously, "Sorry, Detective. Didn't mean to startle you."

Cranston, that was her name. "Never mind, Cranston. What's up?"

Eyes flicked away all around them; Olivia could feel the pressure of so much attention like the pulsing keen of cicadas. She tried to focus on what Cranston was saying.

". . . so I called the LoJack rep the department has been working with, and he sent me a link . . ."

Wait. "Wait, slow down, I missed something. LoJack? That sedan has LoJack?" Every nerve in Olivia's body was suddenly tingling.

Irritation fluttered over Cranston's face. "Yes. LoJack. We have a moving target, but we have it."

Olivia took a deep breath and gathered in the reins of her command. "Let's stop wasting time, then. Load up, everyone! Cranston," she yelled back over her shoulder, "I'm with you."

"One hostile on the way to you, sir."

A short range radio crackled in the small cabin. One of the guards pulled out a small handset from his breast pocket, bent his head to listen.

"Sekhmet is here, Mr. Kroner. The woman, alone."

Kroner grimly shook his head. "Only one of the three I want. Hopefully, she can be convinced to tell us how to find the others."

Eris was thrilled, Ian could tell. She was grinning maniacally, fists clenching and unclenching. In a moment, in just a moment, she chanted, I'll have him. He'll be mine!

Ian knew he should be feeling excitement at the approaching death of his father's killer. It was all he'd wanted yesterday, last night, this morning even. But now he felt as though everything was clearer, the voices gone. He knew that he couldn't know everything, not with the spirit of Discord riding him like a cruel jockey.

He didn't know what to think, other than to know that Eris was at least as dangerous as . . . the other one. Ares. In the body of a woman. It struck him that she could be possessed, too, just like him. Did she really deserve to die?

Eris hissed at him to be quiet. He subsided, wishing he could chew his nails.

The front door slammed open.

Ian yelped in surprise. The small woman entered the room like a movie gunslinger, long coat open, hands at her sides. She seemed unsurprised by her armed welcome.

"Hertzog," she said calmly, "I am afraid you will be disappointed by today's outcome."

Eris bared her teeth. "Ares. You cannot seal me out now."

The woman's cold gaze flicked over Ian, then back to Kroner. She tipped her head back to study him, exposing her neck. The three soldiers behind Kroner exchanged worried glances.

Kroner was still for only a moment, then snapped up his pistol to point directly at the woman's head.

Ian had just a second to react and did it without thinking. He reached into his own mind and pushed Eris aside, just enough so that he could lunge forward and slap the gun from Kroner's hand.

What happened next was a whirlwind. Eris tore Ian away and crushed him, binding him up and locking him behind a mental wall. He could barely see the room beyond.

As though Ian's gambit had been a cue, the woman reached back to the empty air behind her head and pulled out a gleaming, battle-scarred sword. With one smooth sweep, she parted three heads from their bodies. Their blood geysered like fountains and spread across the wooden floor. Eris jumped out of range, leaving Kroner ghost-white and sweating at the point of the impossible sword, its flickering light dancing across his face.

The woman smiled, a sweet, terrifying expression. "I suppose I must deal with your second from now on."

Kroner stammered, "Wh-who are you? Where is my son?"

She tilted her head as though considering her answer. "I am Alexander Sekhmet. I am Ares. I am War incarnate," she said matter of factly, "and your son is dead." With that, she shoved her blade into his chest and twisted. Kroner cried out, clutching uselessly at the obscene weapon jutting from his chest. She watched him slump to the floor with blazing star-bright eyes, lips parted. The entire exchange took only seconds.

Jerking her sword free of Kroner's dead weight, she turned and smiled in Ian's direction. "Eris."

The wall imprisoning Ian was growing blacker by the moment, cutting off sight and sound of the outside world. The last thing he saw was Eris turning from the sword to flee.

With Eris taken to her heels, I was no longer in any true danger. I let her run. I had other ways of dealing with her after this next scene.

Before I could put those plans in motion, I needed to remove my enemies. I was nearly mad with rage and was pleased to have viable targets at which to loose it. I flung the door wide and stepped out into the sunlight, my sword at my side. There was a breathless pause, then the uneven music of gunfire. I brought up my sword with a careless gesture, and the bullets vaporized mere inches from my face. Camilla was hunkered down, as small as she could make herself. I laughed in vindictive amusement at her caution, battle fever rising to a high pitch.

Light and easy, I loped toward the treeline and the nearest man. He was struggling to reload his rifle when I reached him, parting his head from his shoulders with a sizzle and the stench of burnt blood.

Sixteen men left. A radio crackled to my left, and I turned to see three of them, pistols aimed at my head, their legs quaking beneath them. Opening my mouth wide in joyous laughter, I leaped over their fallen brother and spun, Camilla's hard muscles bunching in my shoulders as I cut hands from forearms, slit throats, split one man from scalp to sternum.

By now, I was striped with drying blood, hair springing free to blow in the wind of my passage. Thirteen left, lucky thirteen.

More gunfire, from the south this time, punctuated with shouts in Afrikaans and English. With a wave of my free hand, I brought the bullets under my control and sent them zinging back to their origins. Six men fell silently, seven remained.

Another shout, this one an order to fall back and regroup. My breathing high and ragged, I allowed it. I crept silently behind them until all seven were huddled together, frantically hissing to each other. I sprang on them, three, then four men falling with barely a sound. Yanking a burning hot gun from one dead hand, I stopped before the three that were left, my sword flaming and smoking in a relaxed position atop my right shoulder.

Two men fell to their knees, the spreading wetness at one's crotch stinking of urine. I brought up the gun, put slugs into both men's skulls, and brought both of my weapons to bear on the final man. His hands were raised as though to protect himself, and my finger tightened on the trigger of my stolen gun.

His hands clenched, and he dropped them to his sides. Staring at me, a mad light in his eyes, he spread his arms and said, "I've been waiting for you all my life. Just do it." Sunlight glanced off his bald pate, casting shadows in the creases of his worn face.

Smiling, I dropped the gun. This one deserved the sword.

When the last man fell to the ground with two soft thumps, I took a deep, cleansing, joyous breath, and watched his blood drain into the soft earth.

I sheathed my sword and considered my options as the battle fever waned. Reality left me empty of emotion and trembling with unused energy.

Turning my back on the body at my feet, I released Camilla's tongue. She immediately flared white hot and furious.

"I can't believe I ever thought about working with you. You son of a bitch, those men had no chance!" I was disturbed to see tears on the face she presented me.

I shook my head. "They had no chance, true. But I had no choice." I never did.

Camilla cursed at me. "Fuck you. There's always a choice."

A hollow feeling creeping through me, I shook my head. "You are wrong there. You know it."

"No I don't," she yelled. "They might as well have been ants for all the harm they could do to you. You had choices and you took the easy way out!"

"I have no time for clemency!"

"You should! Those men had lives, families, friends. How can you not care?"

"If you had any idea how many men I have killed—"

"In war, sure!"

"This was war!"

"It was murder!"

She was ruining this moment of pure pleasure. That last soldier, his body behind me, had welcomed his end at my hands, had he not? Was that death not my purpose?

"No it wasn't. Leave humans out of it. Eris is your purpose!"

Eris. By the hell to which I would sentence her, I would deal with Eris.

Camilla burned with righteous fury limned in disgust. She asked, "So now what'll you do?"

Involuntarily, I flinched at the singular pronoun. The memory of Eris' twisted, beautiful face refused to be pushed aside; it was a disturbingly helpless feeling. "There are some benefits to following the rules. If I leave your humans out of it, will you leave me be?"

"I'd sure respect you more."

The car was only a few steps away from the last soldier. I checked my surroundings one more time and got in. Slamming the door of the Mustang with unaccustomed force, I said, "Very well. In this matter, I will go to the authorities."

And gods help us all if the punishment I ask for is authorized.

“No new information, Lieutenant. It’s still twenty-one dead so far as I know.” Cicero waited for a response that wasn’t coming. Olivia barely acknowledged him. She surveyed the carnage surrounding her, thoughts raw and confused.

Most of those dead were armed and armored like a private army, including bulletproof vests and automatic weapons. Several of the dead men had been killed with a sword. A sword, for God’s sake. Her shoulders quivered, and her hands were beginning to shake.

At her hip, her phone buzzed. Olivia jerked in reaction, but managed to pick up the call. It was Hernandez. “Fatunbi,” she responded woodenly.

“Olivia.” The lieutenant’s voice was static-filled, but she could still hear the anger in it. “Lee called in a report for you. What the fuck is going on?”

She drew a halting breath. “I have no idea, Lieutenant. The whole world is sideways.”

Hernandez’s response was a humorless bark of laughter. “No shit.” He paused, then went on in a loaded tone. “Two of the bodies have been ID’d.”

Her ears pricked up. “Dorsey?”

She could almost hear his head shake. “No sign of him. But we do have preliminary confirmation on Hertzog and Wilhelm Kroner.”

What . . . Olivia brought one hand to her aching head. “Kroner is dead?”

“Yes. The coroner thinks he’s been dead a few hours longer than the others, so that’s going to make for interesting paperwork. I’m glad someone got him, even if it wasn’t us.”

That pain was getting worse. “I’ll take it if I have to. Only one of them left to hunt down, then.”

“They are no longer our case.” Each word was bitten off, terse and angry.

The hole in her chest deepened. Olivia snarled, teeth gritted. “Feds?”

“DHS. I’m sorry, Liv, but I can’t hold—”

“Don’t call me Liv.” No one gets to call me that anymore.

A brittle pause. “Right. Olivia, I’m mad, too. But I have to take you off the case. This is going too far up for me to bend the rules, now. Just,” Hernandez sighed, a wordless rush of air that somehow held everything Olivia was feeling. “Just go home. Take a week, work it off in the gym, visit family, whatever. I’m on my way to the site, and I’ll handle what’s left of our case. And I need you to call Kerry.” Quinn’s ex. “Let her know we got his killer.”

If it hadn’t been for that sigh, she might have thrown her phone at a tree. Instead, her knuckles white, she turned and walked back toward her squad car.

“Fine.” She felt a tear drop off her nose and scrubbed at it furiously with her free hand. She closed the connection and settled the phone in her pocket. Time to put this day to rest.

9

Appealing to a Higher Authority

"Where are we going?" asked Camilla. She didn't expect any more answer than she'd gotten the previous nine times, but she couldn't sit still in this much quiet. The countryside flew by steadily as the day crept forward. Alexander had refused to say much of anything, and Camilla had eventually thrown up metaphorical hands on the matter and was sitting back to wait. She restrained herself, but only with an effort.

I don't know what he thinks he's doing, she fumed. For all I know, we're headed to Canada to plead for help from the prime minister.

In a small way, she knew he wasn't telling her so he could feel he was in control, and that sort of petty ploy coming from him should really feel like a victory. Instead, she felt like a heel. It's not as though I had much of a choice; I can't be partners with someone who's planning on killing me, she reminded herself. Besides, after that bloodbath in the park, she really didn't have the luxury of sympathizing with him anymore. She tried desperately to ignore the voice that insisted that if she hadn't tricked him, maybe none of it would have happened. All those people.

Alexander flicked on the blinker and took the upcoming exit, the car slowing to a smooth stop at the end of the ramp. The sign pointing to the right read "Lake Olympus."

"Oh come on. Are you kidding me?" Camilla exploded, "I can't believe no one's figured you people out. You're practically begging for attention from conspiracy nuts." The heavily wooded area was hardly setting up shop on Main Street, but still—Olympus?

He ignored the comment completely, turning the car onto the rough asphalt pointing away from the highway. Camilla felt a pang of unease. What's to stop him from soaking me up right now? I'm really of no use to him anymore.

As the Mustang came back up to speed, she pushed the thought away with an effort. Maybe he was hoping she'd reconsider working with him or she wouldn't be able to keep her mouth shut—that was actually a pretty good bet, given the way he'd seen her behave the past two days. There was really no way for her to know what was going to happen. Whatever he was thinking, she still had a chance at making it out of this bizarre situation as long as she was still alive.

He may have most of the cards, but he doesn't have all of them. And that little confidence booster would have to be enough for now.

The road rumbled underneath the thick tires she'd put on the Mustang last year, and she winced at the thought of how the uneven pavement could be affecting the suspension. Beyond the ten-year-old scotch she'd been wallowing in for the past two years, this car was the only thing she spent money on. The image of well-loved machinery taking a beating from back-country potholes was really hard to think about and probably another control ploy from the stuffed shirt driving her car.

She shunted the train of thought back with difficulty, knowing she couldn't afford to get angry. This was a fight for her life, not a spate of office politics or an argument over a parking space. Her temper went back to a simmer. I'm not done yet, dammit.

The fact that he probably didn't know or care how she felt at this point was biting, and she ignored it as much as possible.

They slowed again, and Alexander took a left, where the road changed abruptly to smooth well-tended concrete. It led down toward a glassy lake she could glimpse through the trees. Something else was there, too, something that glittered more like steel. Camilla wished she could crane her neck to see better.

The drive curved around and opened out into a small parking lot, empty of cars. At the edge of the lake stood a Gothic cathedral of a building, constructed of glass and steel, pointing an immense spire into the sky. The red light of the setting sun reflected off of the tall multifaceted windows, making it look as though it were carved from a monstrous ruby.

"Jesus," she breathed. She felt Alexander glance back to her, almost visibly restraining himself from commenting. The urge to know what this place was, to ask a million questions that would fall all over each other in the haste to be asked was nearly unbearable.

Alexander tightened his grip on the steering wheel and pulled the car into a parking spot. He looked up as he opened the door and stepped outside, and Camilla saw a ring of flagpoles at the edge of the lake that she'd missed in the drive down to the building. Several poles were empty of standards, a few flew flags she'd never seen before, and on one red pennant was raising itself into the wind off the water. The device was a flaming sword.

I scanned the flags to see who was in residence: Conquest, the Hunt, Prophecy, and the Messenger. A full quorum. One worry assuaged, to be replaced by several others.

Minerva's scales crossed with a sword on sky blue was the most encouraging. My full-blood sister would surely side with me, even though our relationship had been strained to near breaking by the Trojan War. We had worked together since our beginnings, general and troops. Besides that, she hated Eris with a cold passion. Minerva would never forgive her for the apple.

Diana and Arawn were wild cards, and their green flag, emblazoned with the image of a Yell Hound in full cry, waved limply, almost coyly at me. On the one hand, the Hunters had never appreciated my rules, indeed, had sided with Eris when I repudiated her. On the other, Diana was almost certain to approve of my new aspect. She would find it highly amusing to see War in a woman's body.

Had Apollo seen all of this? Was that the purpose of Hermes' visit such a short time ago? He was likely to ignore me in favor of his harp and opium, though the oracle represented on his golden pennant was almost certain to be consulted today. Once, he had been very involved in mortal affairs, but the destruction of his oracle at Delphi had soured and turned him inward. Another of my Family whose action I could not predict.

Hermes, as usual, would be as neutral as possible. His blank gray flag fluttered cheerfully as I watched my own raise in residence. I appreciated his fairness, but not when it might turn against me. Eris had good reason to come after me after my treatment of her both when I discarded her ages ago and at my house this morning, and my own case against her was unprecedented. She had attacked me personally, which was against our laws, but she had done it through a human avatar, which could be seen as an acceptable distance if one wanted to split hairs.

I took a breath and straightened my coat, smoothed flyaway hairs back against my skull. I had not visited the citadel in years, had not seen many of my fellows for even longer. I gritted my teeth against the battle before me.

Within, Camilla stirred restlessly. I considered for a moment, weighing politics with her possible reaction to the coming meeting. If I repressed her again, she was likely to become very angry and might even feel driven to launch an assault. While this could be useful in my conflict with her, I could not afford to be distracted before Family, and I certainly would be hard pressed to ignore Camilla's violent objections. If I assimilated her now, I would be weak and exhausted for days if my experience with taking Alexander was typical. I shook my head in frustration and left her as she was.

The citadel's lobby was empty, marble floor gleaming, front desk unmanned. Striding past the front rooms, I pushed open the double doors to the conference room. I stood with a hand bracing each door open, as I surveyed the battleground.

Minerva's human form was the same one she'd had for generations, though she had taken to cropping the iron-gray hair quite short. Large amber eyes blinked slowly at me from an ageless face, then narrowed as she looked past Camilla's body to my bony reality beneath. With a subtle nod, she leaned forward and steepled her fingers beneath her chin. The starched cuffs of her white blazer pulled back to show the warrior's bracers she still kept on her wrists.

As usual, Diana was the first to comment. Her boot-clad feet propped up on the gleaming conference table, she clapped derisively. "That's a new look for you, Mars." Her young face was streaked with bright bars of fuchsia and chartreuse, the lips painted purple, rings piercing the flesh above her brows and circling her small ears. When I'd last seen the spirit of the Hunt, she'd owned a motorcycle, a battered leather jacket, and a sunburn and she had taken to hunting men exclusively. Now, she looked more like a bright bird, though I doubted her prey had changed.

As had been the case for centuries, Arawn stood at her side in a bored, privileged slouch, one hand possessive on Diana's broad archer's shoulder. His colorless eyes were outlined with smudged black kohl, white hair laying in twisted clumps across his albino skin. He smiled at me with a faint spark of approval. The Sidhe's features were sharp, almost insect-like.

"Ares, must you hang about that way? At least come in and close the door." Apollo was ensconced in a gold velvet chaise-lounge near the far wall, gazing out over the lake through the floor-to-ceiling window. I cocked my head warily to him and complied. The red coal at the end of his cigarette flared, illuminating rounded, childlike features and vacant eyes as the doors swung shut behind me.

Standing silent before the huge table, Hermes tugged the cuff of his pale gray suit into perfect alignment and looked me up and down, his opalescent eyes shifting color in a dazzling, kaleidoscopic fashion. The forgettable features gave nothing away.

Breaking her silence like a soap bubble, Camilla spoke. "Jesus, Alexander.

With a family like this, no wonder you're screwed up in the head." Touching her thoughts, I felt the disconcerted amusement behind her words.

Years ago, I would have stifled the laugh I now let roll from my chest, filled with relief at the fellow-feeling in Camilla, anticipation of the battle to come. The air turned icy. Family members are not affected by my laugh the way mortals were, but that did not make it pleasant.

"My Family," I returned jovially, "I rejoice to see you have not changed." Sarcasm hung heavily on my words. I'd never spoken to any of my Family in that fashion, but I found I enjoyed it. That should have bothered me more than it did.

The room had gone silent. I walked to the table, pulled out a chair, and sat. I resisted an urge to swing one leg over the arm of the chair with a pang of concern. That was entirely unlike me, and I shot a searching inward look at Camilla. She seemed to be paying me little attention, focused on Minerva's owlish eyes. This seeming distraction could be a new attack on her part, something more subtle than she'd tried before.

Taking a firm hold on myself, I settled back into the hard office chair. All eyes were on me. I looked back stoically, waiting for them to speak.

Interestingly, though I'd known him to have the patience of a stone, Hermes was the one to break the stalemate. He pulled out a chair for himself and folded his compact body into it. His eyes shifting into a silvery gray, he scanned the room. When his gaze returned to me, he smiled cordially.

"So, brother-cousin," he murmured, "tell us what you want." With a graceful hand movement, he called up two glasses and a bottle of scotch. I nodded in amused appreciation as he poured us both a measure.

Leaning forward, I plucked the tumbler from his outstretched hand, weighing the situation. "You are as perceptive as ever, Hermes." As I had expected, while Apollo may have drifted away from the conversation, even Arawn looked interested now. "I have not come here before without business at hand and do not do so now." I sipped my scotch, flooding my mouth with the taste of smoke.

"I come to ask for judgment on Eris."

"Is everyone gone? Is it just me?"

The voices were gone, entirely fenced away, and he'd never felt so alone in his entire life. It was hard to think in the booming silence of his mind.

You're not alone, he thought fiercely, and that's your main problem right now.

Eris had shoved him aside as though he were a yapping puppy, and it didn't matter whether she was real or a new symptom, this had to stop. He had to regain control. He had to find some way back to the pilot's seat of his body, even if the mind he was fighting was his own. Shivering, he realized that would actually be easier to deal with. Wrestling with the spirit of Discord would be a whole new animal.

He shook off the image as forcefully as he could. He really had to approach the problem as something familiar, something he had some chance of dealing with. So, approach it the way he'd been taught by every shrink he'd ever known. Use imagery to trick the brain into going down the right path.

It was hard to get himself into the right frame of mind for this sort of thing most days, especially with the voices constantly interrupting and distracting him. Today in the echoing silence of his head, it was as simple as taking a few deep breaths. He built a vision of the wall in his mind, circling him like castle battlements, a deep well of a jail cell. He could almost see it, made of odd-sized rocks and thick mortar, thorny bushes keeping him from getting close. It was cold and damp and set him shivering.

"Goal one," he muttered to himself, "is to get out. Goal two is to stay out. Should I climb it or break it?" Yesterday, the voices would have had a say, might even have helped, and he was disturbed to find himself missing them again. He pushed away the thought and searched his surroundings for a tool. There was always a tool. In his past experience with this technique, he'd used his hands, only to have them shredded before he could make a dent in the wall. For whatever reason, he needed to accept the help those tools represented. Once he'd tried to cap all the voices in a prescription pill bottle. Pushing aside that particularly disastrous session, Ian noticed an iron spike hidden beneath one thorny branch, next to a pile of loose rock. He hefted the unfamiliar tools, then aimed the spike at the base of one of the thorn bushes between him and the wall and struck it once with the rock, as hard as he dared. It made a loud thunk. He paused, tense, to see if Eris would appear.

When everything stayed quiet, he struck again, harder. A chip of stone flew past his ear. I can do this, he insisted to himself. I can do this.

Camilla watched, fascinated, as the neon-streaked girl twirled a lock of black hair around her index finger.

"I have been waiting for you to call for judgment on Eris for ages, Mars." Diana looked up at the skinny punk behind her, grinning. "Though I wish you had asked for the Wild Hunt."

Alexander eyed her stonily. "Your support would mean much to me, sister-cousin, did I not remember your position when Eris and I parted."

Diana rolled her eyes. "Things change, man. I got really tired of her ranting." She waved one hand dismissively, the Egyptian asps tattooed on her arms undulating with the motion.

Downing the rest of his scotch in one swallow, Alexander ignored her, focusing instead on the older woman. "Minerva," he said genially, "the question of Justice is set before you, Justice lawfully meted out. Will you hear my plea?"

The inhuman golden eyes shifted, glancing around the room.

I will not think of her as a goddess. This is just too much. Camilla cut herself off. Hysteria wasn't going to help, and neither was denial.

Minerva braced her hands on the table and stood. "In any other plea for Justice, you would be correct, brother. However, I must recuse myself from this matter. I am biased where Eris is involved." A cruel expression moved across her face. "The Erinyes would never take that order from me, much though I wish they would." Alexander's shoulders hunched slightly. Camilla would bet he'd been counting on Minerva's support.

Camilla focused on the tall woman, finally catching a bit of the subtext the room was swimming with. That golden apple Alexander had spoken of, that started the Trojan war—Minerva had been one of the goddesses who wanted it. But who were the Erinyes?

She bit back a nervous laugh. Who knew I would ever need a fucking English major to save my life? This is completely surreal.

Alexander's gaze flicked around the room, giving her little still frames of the faces there. Diana and Arawn, somehow managing to look both bored and speculative. Apollo, his face turned out to the sunset, cigarette trembling in his fingers. Hermes, his eyes now settled on a flat gray that reminded her of primer paint.

Economical of movement, the gray man pushed his chair back and stood, tugging his waistcoat straight. "It appears we'll need to fill out the quorum, Ares." He turned to Minerva with a polite, questioning look. "Who do you suggest?"

The goddess paused as though turning the question round in her head. Camilla realized that Alexander was tapping one foot in an agitated manner and was struck by how unlike him that seemed. Carefully, she reached out, trying to stop the movement.

The foot stilled.

Holy shit, holy shit.

And the best part, Alexander didn't seem to notice. Holding herself as small as possible, Camilla scrambled to bank the spark of excitement flaring in her chest.

Don't let him know, idiot! she hissed to herself. If he knows he's losing control, you're done for.

From the conference table, Minerva nodded decisively. "I name Nemesis to take my place. Please call in the Kindly Ones as well." One shoulder hitched upward. "First though, I want you to inform our remaining siblings. All of the Four should all be involved in this." Her eyes flicked to Alexander and sparkled when he looked away. Internally, Alexander was all fire and flashes, and that could not be a good thing.

Hermes nodded deferentially to her, then turned and left the room without another word.

Camilla was having trouble taking this all in. All these immortal beings, mincing nicely through parliamentary procedure.

The air all around them seemed charged in Hermes' wake. Alexander let out a long, slow breath.

I've passed one hurdle, at least, though this will be a difficult race.

Wait, that was—that was Alexander's thought. Was he talking to her again or were more of the barriers weakening? Camilla felt a rush of anticipation zing through her, and her hands curled into fists. Her real, physical hands. Alexander absently shook them as though they tingled, looking sharply around the room as though at a nest of serpents.

He's distracted, she realized. He could stop me if he were paying attention, I bet. I'll have to be really careful.

Frustrated, she settled herself back, making herself unobtrusive, knowing she couldn't keep it up for long. I don't have much time left.

It was like he was chipping away at dried mud covering a window. Each lump that fell let in a little more light.

He had no idea how long he'd been working on the wall he'd visualized, but Ian was certain he was getting somewhere. If he put his eye up to the hole he'd made, he could see out. It was like riding a rollercoaster, jerks and twists he couldn't control.

Except the coaster was really his head, turning at Eris' direction. He felt a stab of anger and possessiveness. It was his body, his, and she had no right to use him like a set of clothes.

With that thought came a phantom voice, freezing his blood.

Ian, she has to go.

He backed away hurriedly from the chink in the wall, panic wiping away his anger. The voices were out there, waiting for him.

So that's what the price of freedom was. Insanity.

At first, he'd been lonely here in the emptiness of his mind. Sometime during his dig through the wall, he'd relaxed. He could think straight, make plans, carry them through—all without interruption or distraction.

God, could he handle the voices again? Was it worth it?

Dammit, I can't stay here locked up, a prisoner in my own head! He stared across at the tiny hole he'd made in the wall, his own personal window on insanity.

What do I do now?

Diana approached me first, all gangly arms and dark eyes and bright metal studding her flesh. At least my Family was as I'd expected it. In this situation, I was relieved that it was difficult for immortals to change their behavior. I needed every advantage I could find. My Family tended to play rough.

She slid her thin rump onto the table next to me, her coltish legs kicking the air. I winced. She'd never had manners she cared to follow, unless it were some code she'd never explained to me. I was unlikely to know. I was hardly her favorite brother.

"Mars-Alexander!" she gushed, eyes bright with cynicism. "Or do you go by Alexandra these days? Never would have thought you would get a sex change." She was trying to goad me as if I were one of her hounds.

Gritting my teeth, I let it pass. "You may call me whatever you like, sister-cousin. I can hardly stop you."

That surprised a bell-like laugh from her. She leaned forward to slap me on the arm. "You have so relaxed! I think I'll call you Alex. That works both ways." She snorted unbecomingly.

"Yes." Oh, how I'd like to spank that child. And she likely knew that.

Arawn sidled up to us on schedule, fitting himself between Diana's knees. I sighed. Arawn was not immediate family and had never been comfortable in his position as my sister-cousin's consort. I felt the beginnings of a condescending sneer at the corner of my mouth. I gentled it as much as I could.

I shook my head and smiled lazily up at him, making his almond-shaped eyes narrow. "King of the fair folk," I greeted him. I didn't feel like giving him the family title today, even though it would be politic.

The sharp angles of his face could have been carved from stone. "Brother," he said deliberately. Posturing, always posturing. I should be used to it. Time was I used to revel in this type of politics, but that was long ago, and I was beginning to feel a distinct longing for my solitary, safe home.

Camilla sent me a strong, undiluted dose of agreement. She'd heard the thought, one I hadn't intended to broadcast.

With an abrupt, violent movement, I stood, sending my chair skittering and wailing backward like a nervous horse. Camilla also jerked away, but Diana and Arawn were unmoved. They watched as I gave them a perfunctory nod and turned to Minerva. She stood silhouetted against the darkening sky, her owl-eyes reflecting the firelight like pools.

She regarded me as I approached her, a frown twisting her forehead. "Ares," she murmured as I drew close, "this behavior is unlike you, in many ways. Have you truly changed that much so quickly?" Reaching out, she touched my shoulder lightly.

More than you knew, sister. My head was crowded to capacity.

I stopped beside her to look out at the lake. "Desperate times, sister," I said clearly, "and I have not kept pace with them. Few of us have." I felt her attention on me sharpen. "The time will come when our brother will sound the call, when we will wage the final War. I do not wish to be flicking the beads of an abacus or waiting months to know the outcomes of the battles that will come. I must adapt or die."

She was still beside me, the stillness of intense thought. Putting one hand to my elbow, she whispered, "Is that time upon us all? What do you know that you have not shared, brother?"

I shrugged. "We must all at least choose sides. As to when . . . ," I hesitated, then cocked my head toward Apollo, "our brother-cousin may be able to answer that question."

Her reaction startled me. "Bah!" she spat, her face hardening, "There sits one of us who has kept pace with the times, Ares, and has not fared well as a result. He is barely sane, never lucid." She paused and said in a low voice, "May the War begin soon, if that is our only course."

I looked back over the room, returned my gaze to Minerva's face. I gave her a crooked smile and turned to face her fully.

"Diana is not wearing her crown. Does this mean she no longer pilots the moon?"

Minerva blinked at my non sequitur, then glanced over to our sister where she stood blatantly kissing her consort. With a moue of distaste, she turned her back on the spectacle.

"She does not. She's given that dominion to the Fair Folk. Mab wears the crown." Her voice low, she added as an afterthought, "She hunts day and night now." Her dry tone told me clearly what she thought of the matter.

I spread my arms. "So some of us move with times and actually come out ahead, then." When Minerva made as if to speak, her features muddled and confused, I cut her off. "Diana has given away her responsibility to her consort's family and in return has total freedom of movement. Without losing any of her power." My sister's eyes narrowed.

Turning to face my brother, I muttered, "I wonder what Apollo has gained." Perhaps I should find out. Turning from Minerva, I moved toward his dark corner, intending to feel him out.

I stopped short when the double doors opened to admit my brother and sister.

Pestilence swaggered in, an irritating whistle on her berry-red lips. Skin-tight jeans emphasized her emaciated frame. She wore a moss green scarf around her neck and was wreathed in the smells of cigarettes and cheap beer. Her nod to the room was perfunctory, and then she turned to usher in our brother and leader of the Family, Thanatos.

We all bowed. His black suit was cheap and ill-fitted, as though he had outgrown it. One wilted pink carnation adorned the buttonhole. His answering smile was greasy and familiar.

"Death is here, children," he drawled. "We're ready for both the trial and the funeral now."

Ian sat against the back wall he'd so carefully created, visualizing the barrier in his mind so that he had a chance of taking it down. The chink he'd made was no larger and would get no larger unless he went back and chipped the rest of it away.

But how could he? Finally, after years of confusion, he was himself again, just Ian, no bombardment of the opinions and feelings and words of those others who had spoken to him for so long. Could he really give all that up again? Embrace the voices he now knew were waiting for him outside that wall, just to have the chance to get his body back? Was it really worth it?

Was solitary confinement any better?

He felt frozen, as though presented with a million equally awful choices. A pang of longing came over him, a desire to give this decision away, to anyone. He fairly shook with it.

"No," he whispered to himself, "I can make choices on my own. I can!" He looked away from the patch of light, then forced himself to stare directly at it. "And besides, I know I only have one real choice." He would have swallowed hard, had he a throat.

The voices—they were something he knew, something he could deal with. But locked in the prison of his own mind, alone, maybe forever? He'd probably go insane that way, too, though in a more conventional fashion.

No choice is still a choice. Gathering up his courage with shaking hands, he went back to the hole in the wall and resumed his careful destruction. He could see through it clearly, now. Eris was talking with a man, a nondescript, gray man in a gray suit with bright, bright blue eyes.

Ian!

The voices, oh God, they weren't even going to give him a moment's rest.

Lay low.

Be quiet, don't let her hear you!

The Messenger is taking us to him!

To the killer.

You can still avenge your father, Ian!

It was a barrage of voices, hissing whispers, high squeals, low growls. It was overwhelming and strangely welcoming, like a pack of dogs greeting their master. Ian flailed under the assault and cursed frantically. They swarmed over him, surrounding him in a buzz of white noise.

Hunched against their barrage, he began to realize that they weren't attacking him. It felt more like a shield, a constantly moving force field between his mind and the thing that had imprisoned him. They were protecting him, hiding him inside their chaos.

"Give me space, let me breathe," he whispered, his dream fingers knotted around the iron spike.

The constriction eased as the ephemeral swirl grew in diameter. Ian's chest clenched. They had obeyed him.

The voices spun in barely discernible paths between the small breach in the wall and the world outside. Ghosts, hiding him from Eris.

Leave the wall.

Weaken it, but leave it standing.

Then you can choose your moment, Ian!

Ian nodded slowly, then focused on the wall. Take that stone and a few there . . . if he were careful and didn't let it crumble before he wanted it to. It was worth the try. He angled his makeshift chisel and began to work hidden behind the wall and the voices in his mind, and watched from the corners of his eyes as Eris agreed to follow the gray man to a place he called Olympus.

"And I thought I was crazy before?" he huffed to himself as he worked. This story would make some psychiatrist famous if he got himself home.

Death plonked himself in a chair apart from the scattered family members, grinning quietly to himself. Camilla couldn't ignore the feather-light tickling of nausea emanating from him like an aura. She poked Alexander.

"Is he always like that?"

"We avoid his company for good reason."

Hmm. "And Pestilence? Does she have another name?"

"Mary." She was giggling with Diana, two teenagers gossiping. Arawn looked ill.

"Really?"

Alexander bridled at her tone. "This is not a joke, Camilla. We are not a joke."

Camilla let it go. Mary's whistled tune ran in the back of her mind like calliope music.

The doors opened again. Alexander went still. This was the moment Camilla had been waiting for. He was completely distracted.

Unfortunately, so was she.

Leading the group like a herald, Hermes was the first in, his mercurial eyes flashing an acid green. Behind him walked the figure that had frozen Alexander: Ian, his face contorted in an evil, satisfied grin. The expression was completely alien to the young man's face, and Camilla found herself wondering what the poor kid was really like.

Camilla tried to ignore him and gathered herself to fight for the controls of her body and then snared herself again on the faces behind Eris.

A step back from Ian paced a small child, looking maybe two or three years old at the most. Her summery white dress was ragged and torn at the edges, fluttering in an unfelt wind that also brushed coppery curls from her forehead. The small round face was unremarkable until she smiled, the mouth full of an array of sharp pointed teeth that couldn't possibly have fit in the childish mouth. The brown eyes were flat and pitiless.

Camilla might have been able to shrug off the child's gaze, but the figures behind her tiny body froze Camilla solid.

The Erinyes, she thought blankly.

They walked three abreast, advancing like a line of soldiers. The bizarre features were burned into her mind: The woman in the center had high-arching wings folded behind her, fledged with glowing white feathers. To her left marched another woman, her hair swimming with small snakes arching and hissing. The final woman looked completely human except for the tears of blood streaming in an unceasing torrent down her white cheeks. Their faces were identical, as though they'd all been stamped from the same mold.

The whole room was silent, in awe or trepidation, or some god-emotion Camilla couldn't name. Maybe they all just wanted to see who would back away first.

The surreal group paused in the doorway as if to gauge its effect, but Eris pushed past Hermes and strode up to Alexander, eyes never leaving his. She stopped bare inches from him, then her expression twisted and she spat full in his face.

It seemed to wake him from his daze. Without pausing to wipe the spittle from his face, he slapped her, hard.

Eris stumbled back, hand to abused cheek. Camilla found herself grinning madly, shocked and approving.

"Way to go, Alexander!" She couldn't stop the words or the urge to hug him as though he were a teammate. "I can't believe she didn't even see that coming."

"Camilla, stay out of this please." His thought was steely cold, full of something barely restrained. It felt like he'd just slapped her, too, and Camilla sobered with a wince.

With dignified motions, Alexander reached into the pocket of his greatcoat and pulled out a pressed and folded square of linen. Shaking it loose, he mopped his face and turned to face Hermes.

"Brother-cousin," he said, voice quiet and deadly, "Why have you brought Eris to this proceeding?"

Hermes' eyes spun back to the flat gray they'd been before. "She has the right to address the accusation." His shoulders moved in an indifferent shrug. "Besides, the whole affair will be far more interesting with her here." He turned to Thanatos and bowed deeply. Death waved him off, leaning elbows to knees.

"Brothers and sisters, this will be a glorious day!" His black eyes were oily pools of glee.

Camilla felt Alexander's tension creeping into his shoulders. No, dammit, her shoulders! Stop empathizing!

He crumpled his handkerchief and stuffed it back into his breast pocket. With a grand angry flourish, he bowed to the newcomers still at the door. "I welcome you, Nemesis and Erinyes, judge and jury in this matter. May your finding be true and your judgment, swift."

The child laughed, a chillingly normal sound issuing from behind those teeth. All four returned the bow. The child (Nemesis, Camilla realized with an uneasy start) skipped forward to Minerva's side and embraced her. The goddess of

Conquest and Justice didn't seem all that happy about it and didn't return the hug. Nemesis pulled back, staring fondly at her.

"My favorite niece," the child said, amused, "You still fear me." Minerva gazed back steadily, though her face paled.

There was a sudden loud rustle, like a flock of geese taking flight. All eyes snapped to the Furies as the center woman mantled her huge wings and leaped into the air, her sisters on either arm. A section of the wall pulled out, as smoothly as a piece of machinery, and the women alighted there, gazing down at the group in total silence. Like vultures, waiting for something to die.

Nemesis raised her soft childlike arms, commanding the attention of the room.

"Immortals all," she called in a soft, piping voice, "The Kindly Ones are ready to fly. Ares has brought suit against Eris. She has chosen to respond with her own accusations. By dawn, the Erinyes will feast on the heart's blood of one of them."

Alexander took in a long, slow breath, as though he'd seen the possibility but had hoped no one else would. Camilla could feel her hands curl into fists with his reaction, cutting little crescent moons into the palms with the fingernails.

With a childlike jump and joyless, ancient eyes, Nemesis vaulted herself into the nearest chair.

"Let the deposition begin."

At this point, Ian was pretty sure Eris wasn't something his damaged brain had come up with. The confusion of faces around him was bizarre, even fantastically impossible, but those faces were real. Even the Erinyes, wound 'round with serpents and wings and blood. Everything was real.

Ian, did you hear?

Ian.

They will destroy your father's killer!

Destroy, rend limb from limb.

"Shut up," he hissed, and the voices again subsided reluctantly. "Your damn revenge got me into this in the first place, but if you just shut up, maybe I can get out of it!" Though how that was going to happen, he couldn't say. He paused his finicky work on the wall to stare at the characters outside.

He did not want to be hunted by the Kindly Ones. He'd read enough about them, taught everything he knew about them to countless students to know what would happen to his body if Eris lost her suit. A wave of nausea swept through him, remembering how he'd reveled lecturing on the gory details of the legends back when they were just legends.

Beyond his hidey hole, Eris was jubilant.

"You will pay for your broken contract, Ares!" She began a wild little dance, spinning until all Ian could see was a blur of color. Panting, she stopped short in front of the uniformed woman who was also somehow Alexander Sehkmet. Her figure dipped and swirled, resolved to a pained scowl.

"If anyone has broken a contract here, Eris, it is you." The soldier brought one hand to her brow in an oppressed fashion, something old and frustrated in her eyes.

"Be silent!" The little girl brought her fist down on the table, creating a far louder noise than should have been possible. When she had everyone's attention, she called, "Ares, lord of War. State your case."

Sweet Jesus. Lord of war . . . did that mean that Sehkmet had been the god of War? Then why the new body? Was he hiding?

She's like you, Ian.

Trapped, like you.

Ian wanted to put his face in his hands. The gods, the fucking immortals were playing out their petty wars and trampling on men like ants on the battlefield the way they always had. A dry laugh bubbled in his throat with no way to get out.

The woman straightened her shoulders and stepped forward.

"My Family," I began, "I charge Eris with waging war directly on my person, bypassing our law that prohibits conflict except through mortals." I held myself at attention, arms stiff at my sides.

Across the table, Nemesis nodded, her grave expression incongruous on her childlike aspect's face. "Explain, in detail."

I took a slow breath to ready myself. "As is obvious to you all, my human form is new. I have not taken a new one in centuries. In fact, I expected never to take a new one. I was forced to abandon my old incarnation and take a new one by direct action of my former daimona, Eris."

As I had expected, Eris took offense. "Lies!" She spat the word at me, frothing. "You inhabit a mortal, I inhabit a mortal. I have broken no law I recognize!" Mary jumped to her feet, applauding.

"To order!" barked Nemesis. "You will have your turn, Discordia. Keep the peace until then." Eris snarled and subsided.

Camilla was studying Eris intently, as though trying to see past her to the boy she'd possessed. Thankful that Camilla was occupied with something other than me, I ignored the interruption. "Knowing my habits and mind better than anyone else, she manufactured a situation where I had no option but to take the drastic measure of a new body and identity. My current identity is not yet complete, and knowing this, she took a human of her own and confronted me in my own citadel." I gestured angrily toward her. "We all know that should I be destroyed, humanity will be unconstrained by the rules of War. Likely, the rest of our family would follow me to destruction, and only Discord would reign."

The room broke out in a roar. From his place beside Diana, Arawn spoke. "Brother-cousin, I would not have thought you could stoop to acting as a barracks lawyer." His voice was sly and vindictive. The cross-talk grew louder.

Before I could respond, Nemesis again rapped her hands on the table. "Elf-king. Do not attempt to tell us what to rule." The rounded child's face had lit with fury, tiny needle teeth bared. Arawn drew himself up, sharp features lit with inhuman anticipation.

Inwardly, I swore. Should this devolve into a Family spat, Eris was much more likely to prevail. She thrived on public discord and would never hesitate to use the confusion against me. I watched her smile quirk Ian Dorsey's face, and I clenched my fists. Would that I could deal with the elf-king myself, but that would cause even more uproar.

Thankfully, there was no need. Diana snaked her arm around Arawn's neck and dragged him down to her level for a hissing rebuke none of us needed to hear. When she released him, Arawn was silent, his face drawn in lines of anger and resentment. He'd lost more face than he'd thought to gain with that attack. I wondered why he took such chances.

With an air of satisfied authority, Nemesis turned back to me. "And when Eris confronted you?"

Brought back to the task at hand, I couldn't keep the slow grin from my face. "I struck her and threw her out of my house."

The Family's amusement made the room ring. Diana laughed delightedly. "Alex! I should hang out with you more often." Arawn twitched violently behind her, and she ignored him. I began to relax, feeling the tide of approval swinging my way.

"It will cost you, brother-cousin." Apollo's tired voice was unexpected, chilling the echoes of laughter. "It will cost all of us."

Voices went silent. Every face in the room swung to his corner, like iron filings to a magnet. I felt a trickle of sweat run between my shoulder blades, my tension returning full-fold.

Nemesis broke the silence, turning her face to the darkness. "Nephew," she said, her words oddly gentle, "What do you mean? What is this cost?" Her tiny brow was furrowed.

Apollo stood and made his languid way into the pool of light centered on the conference table. His face was puffy, the eyes dark and inward-turned. "His choices will lead us to the next Great War," he murmured, taking a drag from his nearly finished cigarette. "To survive it, we will all have to change beyond reason, beyond belief."

Behind me, Minerva broke the spell Apollo's words had cast with a long-suffering sigh. "Brother-cousin, be clear or be silent. You interrupt us with your vague warnings. Ares is the lord of War, his nature and duty is to bring us to the Great War. This is no news to any of us."

Mary cupped her hands around her lips. "Sit down, you daft bastard!" Arawn cheered her, and when I risked a glance in his direction, I saw an array of the Sidhe at his feet, cheering with him. Our audience was growing.

Pinching out the coal of his cigarette, Apollo flicked his fingers to produce a new one, already ablaze. "Sister, you misunderstand. The era of immortality is near its end. We are near our end." His voice was flat, his fingers trembled.

I broke into the thick fog of disbelief clouding the room, a hollow feeling growing in my chest. "How does this follow from my actions, brother-cousin?"

He looked directly at me, despair in every line of his face. "None of us will survive the War that is coming, Alexander. And you and your daimona will be the first of us to fall."

Camilla felt as lost as she knew Alexander felt, as though his emotions were bleeding into hers. Apollo talked like a drug addict, but his family hung on his every word like worshipers at a tent revival. Slowly, they all turned to look at Alexander, fear and accusation aimed directly at him.

To his credit, Alexander didn't back down one iota. He squared his shoulders and addressed Apollo politely, though Camilla could feel the restraint that required. "What are you suggesting? All of us, all the immortals, we will die?"

Apollo shrugged. "Yes, we will. In one fashion or another."

The room erupted. Alexander twitched as though a fly had landed on his face. Across the room, Diana stood with a catlike grace and shoved her way between bodies to grab Apollo's shoulder. She swung him around to face her, and not gently.

"Can we prevent this?" The girl's voice was tight, sliding up the scale and becoming shrill. "If the War is prevented—if the mortals are forced to wage their own war—" Camilla could practically hear the lower-case "w." It was pretty obvious where the little bitch was heading. So much for getting her support.

The group of immortals rumbled thunderously. Hands moved to belts, boot tops, knives, and swords appearing as if by magic. Actually, probably by magic.

Camilla thought numbly, They're going to kill him. Kill me. Her situation had gone from tenuous stalemate to seconds from execution.

With a nearly audible crack, Camilla felt Alexander's restraint break. He reached up and back, as though grabbing something hanging from one shoulder, then pulled. Something filled his hand, and the others were backpedaling.

It was his sword, glorious and flaming crimson.

Oh crap.

Beyond the bloody light, someone (Nemesis?) gave a surprised, outraged cry.

"Ares! You cannot!" The little girl-shape leaped to the surface of the table, hands outstretched as though she could keep them all apart.

Alexander cut her off with a guttural roar. "Will you kill me before the very eyes of the Kindly Ones? Do you think they will spare you, cowards?" He swung the sword up as though about to strike. The blade sizzled as it cut the air. "If I must die, I will take you all with me to the hells, by the End I promise it!"

The moment stretched. The faces staring back were hung with indecision and fear.

Again Nemesis pounded the table in front of her. The room jumped guiltily.

"Come to order!" she yelled. "Ares, put up your sword and come to order!" Alexander, reluctance in every line, did as she commanded. When the sword winked out of existence, the growing crowd of beings settled again, their voices rising and falling like leaves.

Nemesis surveyed the room, arms braced on her knees. "I remind you, all of you, that as the oldest member of this quorum, I lead and judge in this matter. Should procedure be broken again, I will not hesitate to use this position to enforce order. You will not face the Erinyes, but you may take a turn on Prometheus' rock or in Loki's chains. Do you hear me?"

Through all this, Thanatos had not moved from his slouch. He now waved a disinterested hand. "Children, heed her words. I made these rules, and I will not halt their consequences, much as it may sadden me to lose some of my fine Family." He made a gape-toothed smile. "There are other Families, after all, from whom I can recruit."

Minerva stood. "You cannot replace us, brother."

"That I can't," he agreed. "But even if you all die, I still win."

The crowd pulled away from him. Minerva regarded him levelly. She nodded once and returned to her seat.

"Proceed, please." Thanatos slicked back his coal-black forelock and grinned at the charged and silent room. Nemesis bared her needle-teeth at him in what could have been thanks and turned to Eris.

"Eris. Present your defense and counter suit."

Alexander reluctantly ceded the floor to Eris, positioning his back against the wall next to the doors. Camilla swallowed hard.

The goddess of Discord took his place. Her eyes sparked with anticipation. "Nemesis," she said earnestly, "I am the victim, not Ares. I was wronged long ago and was given no chance at revenge." She pointed at Alexander with one well-gnawed fingernail. "He knew my nature when we contracted as lord and daimona, and I knew his. Nowhere in that contract was there a stipulation for loyalty during Family games! In fact, my challenge to the Greek gods was furthering his own ends. It brought about one of the greatest wars of the era, the Trojan War. I had thought to please my lord! Can I help that he chose the losing side?"

A full-throated bellow greeted her words. The huge room was now full to bursting with gods, and half of them were cheering for Alexander's head. Camilla's head.

"This will not be easy, Camilla," he murmured. "I am sorry to have dragged you into it."

"Even after today's mess?"

"Even so." His smile felt gentle, for the first time not leaving a burning on her lips.

When the noise died down, Eris went on. "I was wronged then, and I am wronged now. So I played a trick on him! Do we not all prick each other until we bleed? Do we not squabble amongst ourselves? I damaged his human persona, not the person of the lord of War! He chose to take another body, not I! And when I took human form myself to confront him, now that I had his attention, he threw me out against all laws of hospitality!"

The rumble this time was significantly darker. Alexander glared.

"Hospitality laws are a big deal, huh?" Camilla shivered at the antipathy in the room.

"Extremely big."

Ian's slim body turned to face Death. "These are laws you set for us yourself, Eldest Brother. Do you agree your brother has transgressed?"

Thanatos rolled his bright eyes. "I highly doubt that War invited you into his castle with bread and salt, dear sister-cousin." A roll of laughter greeted his words.

Eris' nostrils flared. "The spirit of the law was broken!"

"If the Greeks did not break host law at Troy, then War did not break it here."

Her mouth worked around silent curses. Eris snarled and turned her back on Death.

"Nemesis, even given that biased ruling, I am still not guilty of breaking the treaty!"

Alexander gave a low whistle. "She's backpedalling, isn't she," whispered Camilla.

"She is indeed," he said. She could feel his heart lifting.

Eris clearly could feel it too. She pushed harder. "Again and again we go back to the blasted war at Troy. Very well, here is another analogy. At Troy, the gods resolved a quarrel by choosing human game pieces and agreeing to let that determine the victor. Is this not what I did as well? I merely wanted his attention."

She continued over the angry noise she had generated, shouting now. "I did not fight Ares myself. I merely spoke to his servant and turned him with words. Before I sought to speak to Ares, to heal that old wound, I had not brought us into contact at all. If anyone is guilty of starting hostilities, it is him!"

Alexander shifted against his wall and allowed himself to smile. Eris saw it and opened her mouth to spit more politely phrased vitriol.

This time, Nemesis stopped her. With one more bang of her little hand, she brought everyone's attention to her. The packed room was silent.

"I have heard enough." Nemesis looked across the room to the other four members of the jury. "What say you, Hermes?"

His eyes spun like pinwheels. "You come to me before the deciding vote?"

She glared back at him, large eyes lifeless as salted earth. "I am the deciding vote. I merely hear your advice."

"Well then." Hermes shrugged. "This weathervane follows the prevailing wind. I cast my vote for Ares."

The crowd vented its approval. Only a few scattered clots hissed. Alexander drew a deep breath and relaxed his shoulders.

"Diana, Arawn?" What, Diana basically gets two votes? How could that be fair?

"None of this is truly fair, Camilla."

She paused. "What happens to Ian if she loses?"

The silence was answer enough.

Diana allowed Arawn to lift her to her feet. "We vote for Alex. Right babe?"

The Sidhe's eyes burned. "Of course, my love."

The Fae bounded onto the floor with glee. Eris cursed as they wove rings around her.

"Apollo?"

The noise died down somewhat as attention turned to the god of Prophesy. He sighed heavily and lit another cigarette. "Much good may it do you," he muttered. "Ares has my vote."

All eyes moved to Nemesis.

"Eris," she said from her high place on the table, "Your arguments are more ordered than your nature, but they are built on sandy foundation. You began this most recent quarrel that indeed nearly broke the treaty that keeps all the gods safe."

Eris' face tightened.

"I judge for Ares in this matter. Take yourself to the Kindly Ones for your doom."

Eris shrieked, a wild, insane sound, and flung herself across the room at Alexander.

10

Breaking Loose

Sword once again in hand, I hesitated for a fraction of a second. It was enough. She got inside my guard and went for my throat, Ian Dorsey's fingers crooked into bony talons. I fended her off with my free hand, bringing my sword around for a final blow.

And unlooked for, found Camilla blocking my way.

"No!" she grated, her face twisted with outrage. "This kid didn't do anything to you! You killed his father, and maybe he deserved it, but you can't kill him. I won't let you!" The surge of maternal protectiveness she felt for the human boy shook me.

My left hand locked about Ian's throat, I was breathless with rage. First Eris, now my family and Camilla both defied me. I roared and bore Eris to the ground to kneel upon her chest.

"Alexander, no! Please! He's just a boy!" The panicked thought Camilla sent me was full of memories of comrades in arms in the Middle East, dust-coated children counting the days until they could go home to their mothers.

"He's a person, just like me, like you too, for chrissake! What did he ever do to you or anyone you love?" Her mind was full of images of dead people littering the streets of Baghdad. People who had done nothing but live in the wrong place. I had millennia of similar images in my own memory and for the first time, I felt my heart constrict.

It stopped me cold, forced me to see past my battle fever, past Eris, down to the terrified young human locked away from his own body, surrounded by the voices of his illness.

War does not care about the innocent, it is pure conflict. But it can also be the struggle between right and wrong. And this boy had done nothing to me.

I carefully pushed Camilla aside and let go of Ian's throat. "Please relax, Camilla. I will not hurt him." She fell back warily, ready to jump in again should I be lying to her. I glanced up to my Family, all watching our antics in reluctant fascination.

Teeth grinding, I spat, "None of you will take this mortal man without damage."

Camilla focused on Eris lying beneath me, wearing Ian's flesh like a shroud. "You are not going to win this, bitch." She spoke aloud.

Oh Camilla, your timing was as poor as ever. She had regained control, my sword smoking in her hand.

She laid her free hand on Ian's chest, Eris writhing and spitting within him. Within Ian's mind, something broke. The cat-slitted amusement slid from his face, replaced by a fear-streaked anger. Now this boy had pushed aside Eris.

These were not inconsequential vessels. How did I miss this for so long?

"Leave me be!" Ian's voice wrapped around the power inherent in Eris's voice. With an immense effort I could feel, Ian cast Eris from his body. Her essence poured from Ian's gaping mouth and hung as a formless mass of energy and smoke.

Camilla, wielding my sword like a baseball bat, struck Eris. Where the blade should have swept easily through the spirit form, it instead connected and forced Eris into a human shape I remembered well. The warm amber of her skin, the wine-dark hair, the slit-pupiled eyes, but somehow none of it stirred me as it once had. Eris fell to the floor, hissing. Camilla held my sword like a fencing saber, the heavy blade barely bending her wrist. When Eris scrambled to her feet, Camilla shifted her grip to a two-handed style and bent her knees. The spirit of Discord screeched and launched herself at Camilla, talons extended. At the last possible second, Camilla sidestepped and swung the sword in a blurring arc that caught her opponent with the flat of the weapon and catapulted Eris into a wall. She came to rest beneath the Erinyes perched on their ledge.

Eris snarled, "Nemesis, will you not end this farce? Is this not proof enough of War's unfitness for you?" Her breath came fast and ragged.

The child-faced spirit of retribution blinked slowly, and then raised her gaze to her own weapons standing still on the wall.

"I rule, Eris, when I see proof," she said. "Indeed, I have seen enough." Raising one soft arm, she motioned to the Furies.

Tisiphone, she of the bloody eyes, responded with a gleeful, ululating call. Her sister Megara hissed in union with her snakes, and Alecto stretched her wings wide, swinging both of her sisters to her wide back.

They stooped, and I knew fear and despair as I never had.

But they did not stoop for me.

Alecto's arms snatched Eris from the floor and pulled her close. Strong wing beats cracked the air, and the spirits of Vengeance took the spirit of Discord away. Eris' inhuman cry faded into the distance.

My lover, my daimona, was gone.

Eris was gone. Ian's hands clenched into victorious fists. His body was his own again. Disbelieving, he laughed and opened his eyes.

The woman was standing beside him, the point of her sword touching the ground and swaying with her panting breath. The other figures around him had fallen back to give them a circle of empty space. He felt like he laid at the center of a bomb strike.

"Farewell Eris, spirit of Discord."

All heads swiveled to stare at the bloated figure of Apollo as he clapped once, twice. "Hail to Ian Dorsey, spirit of Discord."

The woman snapped an intense gaze to him, her eyes wide, the sword still flaming in her right hand. One by one, the immortals turned again to Ian, understanding dawning.

Ian felt his knees turn to water, and he turned his face to the floor. He spread his hands on the cold marble, as though it could steady him.

"Jesus," he whispered.

I was poleaxed by what had happened. Camilla was bleary with shock, her hold on her body tentative. I reached out to nudge her aside, my senses still reeling. It was enough to pull her mind back to the present. "No, Camilla." I pushed her back none too gently, and she cursed, panic rising in her.

"I cannot allow you to drive me out." I was courteous enough not to explain that she could never drive me out completely. Or could she? If Ian had removed Eris by himself, could Camilla push me away?

No. That cannot happen. I am more than Eris was. My brother rules us all. I know I am stronger than some minor Family member. I knew the thought was hubristic, but can truth be arrogance?

Watching her twist and fight even now, her indomitable nature undeterred by the reality of her situation, I realized that somehow, in all the conflict and strife of the past few days, I'd grown to like this woman, even respect her. She was wasted as a mere lieutenant in humanity's army.

With that one thought, a new possibility emerged—one that could save us both, though we would both lose much, too.

She appeared to feel my revelation, stepping back warily from the tangle of my thoughts.

"Camilla. I think I have discovered an answer to both our problems." The words came hard for me.

Camilla's eyes widened. She thought she knew what was coming. Panic filled her, tinged with anger and shame.

"Fine!" she yelled, her face twisted. "You go ahead and eat me like an afternoon snack, you bastard! You know I can't stop you. I know you don't give a shit about me or what I want, whatever your little polite protests are."

I sighed. "Camilla." I might have foreseen this reaction and spared her the fear. I put up my hands as though to fend her off and simply let go of my hold on her, let go of everything. The feeling was strange, as though I were shrinking.

She was weeping now, tears of frustration and anger. "There's so much left to learn, so much more I could do, but you go ahead and take it away. I hope it chokes you!" A tear ran into her mouth, salt on her tongue. She reached up to swipe at her runny nose and stopped, spellbound. Internally, I smiled. My last, small war was over.

She was controlling her hand. She waggled the fingers, stared dumbstruck when they responded. She glanced over to her other hand, still holding the sword. The length of red-hot steel should have dragged her human hand to the ground, but it seemed no heavier to her than the fencing sabre she'd used at West Point. She stared at it dumbly.

"I surrender to you, Camilla." The words were so bitter, but necessary.

Camilla leaned against the granite wall at her back, knees quaking. Breathing hitched and shallow, her eyes flicked frantically from one immortal face to another, my Family gathered around her like jackals. She kept the flaming tip of the sword leveled at them all. Beside her, Ian was still on hands and knees, staring blankly at the floor.

"Alexander," she panted, "I don't understand." The words echoed and she flinched at the rolling sound.

Across the room, Apollo swept a bow in her direction. "Hail," he called, "To Camilla, the spirit of War."

"No," she whispered. "Oh fuck no. Alexander, you can't—"

"I have. It's the only thing that will save us both, Camilla." I knew I sounded exhausted and empty to her. I hoped heartily this was the right decision, because somehow I knew I couldn't rescind it. She shook her head, still disbelieving.

Beyond the confines of my head, someone snarled, a rolling growl that snapped Camilla's attention back to the room and the people in it. The ring around her had tightened. Diana was at the forefront, her pale face twisted with grief and fury.

"Mortal," she hissed, fingers bent into claws, "I don't know how you did it, but you are a fool to have killed my brother. Now, you are no Family to us! The Erinyes have no jurisdiction. We can kill you without risk." A wicked-looking knife trembled in her hand.

Camilla raised the sword, bracing herself. "I didn't kill him!"

Diana steadied her hand. "There is no other way you could be the spirit of War, mortal."

"Dammit, he's still here! I don't know what's going on, but he's still here in my head, useless as ever." She cast her gaze about, landing on my brother.

"Death!" she called. "Did you take him? Is Alexander dead? Wouldn't that be you breaking your damn treaty?" She shook her sword until the flames flickered.

The room quieted. When eyes turned to Thanatos, he held up one hand. "I have not broken the treaty, children. I don't think I will be collecting anyone else here today."

Minerva pushed to the front of the mob. "I know my brother well, he would never desert his place." Oh sister. I should never have quarreled so long with you.

Camilla brought the sword's point to bear directly on her. "Listen! He's not gone, he's still here in my head. I'm in control now, but I didn't kill him!" Camilla shook her head. "He surrendered to me." The last sentence came out in a grating whisper.

Understanding dawned on Diana's face, wiping away the grief, but not the anger. "He's renounced his powers to you." She coughed out a laugh devoid of humor. "And I can't kill you without killing him, which would bring the Erinyes down on my own head."

Inside Camilla's head, I chuckled. "Now you see, sister-cousin."

I felt a rush of giddiness run through Camilla. She threw back her head and laughed. It was a huge, rolling sound, the crack and bellow of thunder, the crash and boom of a bomb collapsing a building. Loud enough for me to hear, she thought, Good god, the bastard even gave me his laugh. I laughed with her.

Diana winced, then spun and punched the window beside her. It shattered into pieces with a resounding noise, raining shards down on the immortals. Camilla pointed out the family resemblance between Diana and me, and I wanted to laugh again.

With barely a glance at the mess she'd made of the window and her hand, she crossed over to Apollo and grabbed a fistful of his shirt.

"Who's next? You drug-addled idiot, who is next? How do we stop this?" She shook him to punctuate each question, her face frantic.

Apollo smiled humorlessly. He brushed her off with a gesture that sent her flying back into Minerva, who made no attempt to steady her.

"Sister-cousin," he said, a little madness glittering in his eyes, "I've spoiled enough surprises for one day." He bared his teeth in a very unfriendly grin.

I stirred, attracting Camilla's attention. "Sheathe your sword, Camilla. You don't need it anymore."

Hysteria still bubbling, Camilla fought down a giggle. "And I do that how? I'm a little new at this." Her voice was still tinged with barely restrained panic.

I shook my head impatiently. "Relax."

Her eyes bugged, anger starting to warm her frozen fear. "You relax! I never signed up for this!" A drop of sweat ran into her eye. She blinked it away quickly.

"Nevertheless, you have it. You must learn to live with it." Before she could respond, I added, "Bring the sword up behind you and slide it down, point first. When it stops, let go." I kept my voice low and soothing.

Grumbling, eyes narrowed, she complied. As soon as she let go of the hilt, the light from the flames vanished. I felt a twinge of possessiveness and shook it off. The sword of War was no longer mine.

Camilla spoke out loud. "So. Now what?" Realizing she was still crouched down, she stood up straight, settling the heavy coat more easily on her shoulders. Shifting uncomfortably, she thought, I'm going to strip off this get-up as soon as possible. I feel like a little girl in Daddy's clothes.

I chuckled at her thought, but didn't respond. It wasn't my place to tell her what to do. Or anyone else, for that matter. It felt oddly pleasant.

Camilla surveyed her new Family warily, gripping me with a chilled thought when she saw that the room was far emptier than it had been earlier. Diana and Arawn had vanished with their entourage. The gods who had sneaked in earlier were gone. Nemesis was seated in a wooden chair, her face turned up to face the sky, and Apollo had returned to his darkened corner, leaving only Hermes and my full-blood siblings facing us.

Camilla barked out a breathy laugh. "So these are my new in-laws." Minerva winced, but a reluctant smile tugged at her lips. Collecting herself, she bowed to Camilla, then Ian.

Thanatos clapped his long beefy hands, the sounds echoing off the walls.

"You have a new sister, Conquest." His toothy smile didn't reach his eyes. "I wonder who's next. I'm hardly likely to take myself off to Hell, after all."

"You won't have a choice." Apollo sent this barb without rancor. My brother glared back at the Prophet.

"Bastard thinks he can have the last word. Bullshit. I get the last word, always." He stormed out before anyone could prove him wrong.

An awkward silence fell. Minerva turned to look at Apollo, but spoke to us. "Siblings," she said, "if Prophesy won't answer us, we need to find another way. He doesn't hold all of the keys." She grimaced. "We should contact the rest of the Families, even the ones who reject our overtures. I don't believe our fate is set in stone."

"Our brother is alive, if you call it that," agreed Pestilence. She'd moved from whistling to gum-snapping. Camilla glared at her.

Minerva ignored them both. Head turning bird-swift to Hermes, she said, "Messenger, please inform the rest of the Family of these events. I suggest we meet here as soon as is convenient for all of us."

"Yeah," drawled my sister Mary. "You let me know. I'm easy to get a hold of." Winking one long-lashed eye, she too strolled out the door.

The shared eye roll was barely noticeable. Minerva nodded to us, pasted on a maternal smile, and moved to crouch next to Apollo's chair, speaking in low indecipherable tones.

Ian still sat on the floor, now with his back against the wall and a vacant look in his eyes.

Looking sidelong at his wan face, Camilla asked under her breath, "Alexander, is Eris really—"

"Dead. Soon, anyway. It was unmistakable." I paused, feeling a strange mixture of relief and regret. "The Furies had made judgment. They claimed her, at the end."

"And that made him the new Eris?" Graceful as ever.

"Ian appears to have taken up her mantle, in some way. The power, at any rate." My thought grew introspective. The age of immortals. "But perhaps, not her lifespan." I wondered what that meant for the two of us.

Though Camilla was a strong person, she was reaching her limit. "If Eris had to die for him to get her position, why am I 'the spirit of War' when you're still hanging around in my head?"

I laughed, enchanted to find the emotion warm for the first time in my experience. "I renounced my position in your favor and gave it to you willingly." I decided a bit of sly humor might help. "Though I would like to apply for the position of advisor."

Ian flinched hard when Camilla touched his shoulder. I felt her gruff concern for the boy and smiled.

"You will be an excellent warlord, Camilla." Her cheeks flushed.

"I'm not sure I should be happy about that. Ian," she said gently, hooking her hand under his arm and helping him up, "we should get ready. We've got a meeting to prepare for."

Ian scanned the room, stuffing his shaking hands into his pockets, pulling away into himself. "I don't understand. What happened? Who are you?"

Camilla sighed. "You know, I'm not really sure of that anymore."

Ian shot a glance at her, seeming to recognize something in her voice. "Eris is gone. What happened?"

I sat back in Camilla's mind, suddenly seeing why Eris chose this boy in the first place. "Camilla," I murmured, "He has schizophrenia. I think that is part of what attracted Eris to him. It may also be why he has retained her powers." Considering, I wondered if this would be the fate of all of my Family—doomed to pass on their aspects to the human race.

The era of immortality is almost over. I thought back again to Apollo's words and wondered.

Ignoring my musing, Camilla clapped Ian on the arm. "I'm not too sure of that either. I think we're going to have to figure things out for ourselves."

She smiled, and Ian warily smiled back. I raised one eyebrow at her, and she shook her finger at me.

"If you quote one word from Casablanca, Alexander, I'm going to slap you."

I held my peace, but my point was made.

Epilogue

The gym had become less bitter in the past week. Olivia had decided she needed the place and that she wouldn't allow her discomfort to keep it from her after leaving without even opening the door the first time. It wasn't the same after Quinn's murder, but it was far better than staying home watching DVDs of Buffy the Vampire Slayer day and night.

There was no one to hold the heavy bag for her today, so she was on the weight machine when Camilla Sykes walked in.

"Hey, Olivia." Her angular soprano was somehow darker today. Olivia detached her grip from the bars of the machine and sat up slowly to eye the army girl.

"Camilla." She'd spent hours in the last week planning this very conversation, full of bitter quips and jabs that would make Camilla squirm and beg for forgiveness. Now, all she could get out was the woman's name.

She flicked her eyes at the ceiling for a second and refocused on Olivia. Her gaze was frank and determined.

"I'm going to be out of town a lot for the foreseeable future, Liv. I didn't want you worrying."

Don't call me Liv. Wiping sweat from her brow, Olivia gave Camilla her best blank stare. "Why would I worry?" She levered herself to her feet as she unwrapped her hands and moved off toward the locker room. "We're not lovers, we're not close friends. I barely know you."

"I'd really like to change that." When Olivia raised an eyebrow, Camilla grimaced. "I know. You have no reason to trust me. And you're probably in no mood to put up with trying."

Olivia stopped to look Camilla up and down. There wasn't any one thing about her that made her different. Her hair was pulled into a low ponytail at the nape of her long neck, a white t-shirt over soft pants, and the combat boots that had first caught Olivia's attention months ago.

"I really did want you, Cam. But I know you don't want that from me, and I don't know what you do want." Something was different. Had she worn makeup before?

"I just want a friend, Liv. Someone who will miss me when I'm gone, who's glad to see me back." Camilla chuckled. "Someone as completely human as you are."

That . . . that was different. Her voice, even her laugh was so much more relaxed now. Camilla's shoulders had always been bunched up around her ears, but now she looked calm and in control.

"You can't tell me anything about this? Where you'll be, what you're doing?" Dammit, was she really going to fall for this?

Camilla's smile opened into a heart-stopping grin, and it sent a pang through Olivia's chest. "Sorry, not a thing. You wouldn't believe me anyway."

Olivia waved that off, fighting back a reluctant smile. "Oh, don't you throw that at me, 007. Don't you be putting on airs. Or I'll have to knock a lot of sense back into you when you visit me."

She could see Camilla fighting to master her expression. Finally straight faced, she stuck out her hand.

"Deal." They shook on it.

END

About the Author

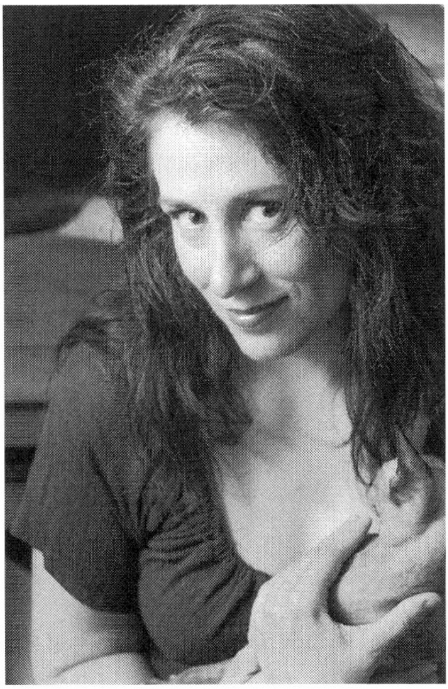

Aimee Kuzenski lives in northeast Minneapolis, MN. She moved there in 1996 in an effort to use her BFA Acting Power for good, and discovered she didn't really enjoy having no health care and looking for a new job every four weeks. After some discussion and internal musing, Aimee took to the University of Minnesota for electrical engineering training. The final result seems to be a blending of the two extremely different disciplines. By day, she works as a technical writer for a local engineering company. For much of the rest of the time, she sits in her home studio and writes fantasy, science fiction, and her own blend of the two.

Aimee also trains in eskrima, a Filipino martial art. She believes hitting things with sticks is both beautiful and therapeutic.

The breathtaking saga continues with...

To Break My Enemies

By Aimee Kuzenski

Read on for an exciting excerpt from the next book in the series coming from Bookmen Media Group in Summer 2014.

To Break My Enemies

On sale Summer 2014

1

Setting the Chessboard

Minerva Price, spirit of Conquest and successful commodities broker, scanned her tablet, moving nothing but her owlish yellow eyes. Oil was soaring above $150 per barrel, gold hovering stagnant at $1700 per ounce. Earlier that week, Pestilence had hinted at a drought she would cast at the American grain belt for this summer. On the strength of this tip, Conquest had purchased several large blocks of food staples the previous day. Her move stimulated the market, and the prices were already up.

A window popped into the center of her screen, obscuring the blinking numbers. An IM from her assistant.

Camilla Sykes for her lunch meeting, Ms. Price.

The smile on Minervas lips soured, a worm of disquiet wriggling in her gut. War's apprentice moved quickly. There had been no meeting scheduled as of yesterday. The Family hadn't known of Sykes existence before yesterday. Minerva typed out a quick affirmative and settled herself with the windows at her back. Looking down the long walkway to her desk, she knew she looked imposing. It should help set Sykes back on her heels.

For the entirety of Minerva's existence, her brother Ares, the spirit of War, had been her near-constant companion. A few millennia ago, their relationship had tripped over War's priggish sense of honor, and they'd parted ways in a huff that then matured into a deep crevasse neither had been willing to bridge, though their duties remained unchanged. She saw him on and off, enough at least to notice when he assimilated the body and personality of Alexander the Great. After that, her normally implacable brother developed a temper to rival Alexander's own, and even adopted his name amongst mortals. Now Alexander Sekmet, he developed a secret reputation as a premier weapons dealer, in the same way that Minerva cultivated the persona of a stock broker.

The Family of gods. Ruled by the quadumvirate of the Horsemen, was shaken to its splintered core yesterday, when Ares arrived at their American citadel on Lake Olympus, wearing a new body and demanding judgment upon Eris, the spirit of Discord, and Ares' former lover. Eris forced Ares into a new body and challenged him openly, thus breaking the treaty between the gods that kept them all from destroying each other.

Conquest shifted minutely in her chair, considering these things as she watched the door to her office. The new body had been a surprise, the suit against Eris an amusement, but the shock had been the realization that the previous occupant of that new body, Camilla Sykes, was still there, locked behind the bars Ares erected to keep her there. Normal practice was to either evict or absorb the mortal soul immediately on possession.

The trial became a circus within moments of the Furies' arrival . More and more members of the Family crept into the citadel, until it was thick with immortal breath. Eris had shown up wearing the body of a young man—another mortal— and she also allowed her new host to remain in his own head. And at the climax of the trial, when prevailing winds had blown against Eris—the fool goddess lost control of her host. The mortal boy tore her from his body, to be snatched up by the Furies and borne away to her ugly fate.

Then, in an ambush move that Minerva neither understood nor trusted, Apollo, drug-addled god of prophesy, declared the young mortal to be the new spirit of Discord. Pressing the point with the dark joy of a man thrusting a dagger into his enemy's vitals, Apollo told the entire assembled Family that our fate was to die and be subsumed by the mortals we rule.

Surely, Eris would have gloried in the pandemonium that statement caused.

Gods suddenly facing the prospect of mortality—a hall of terrified infants could not wail more loudly.

In the midst of this ruckus, Ares did something Minerva thought beyond him. In fear for his existence, Ares relinquished his office to Camilla Sykes. He stepped back to cede control of Camilla's body, and Apollo hailed her as the new spirit of War.

Today, this woman would walk into Conquest's office as War, with Ares riding pillion in her mind.

The large doors across the office opened, and Camilla strode in. For a small woman with unremarkable features, she took command of her space well. Spine straight and expression confident, she ignored the numbers scrolling and blinking on screens set at eye level. She had eschewed the army uniform she'd worn at the Family lake house, dressed now in jeans and riding boots. The sleeves of her button-down shirt were rolled up above her elbows and her dun-colored hair fluttered loose around her ears.

Minerva rolled her shoulders infinitesimally to relieve some tension. Sykes was entirely calm, and Minerva should have expected that. Her brother most likely whispered in her ear. Cautiously, Conquest manufactured a lazy smile as she watched War trek the rest of the long distance to her desk. When Camilla reached an acceptable distance, Minerva drawled, "Have you been practicing your riding, Horseman?" I will put you off balance if I have to sweep your legs from under you, girl.

Camilla stopped short and bit down visibly on her response. More of Ares' doing, no doubt. When their eyes met, Conquest could almost see her brother behind them.

Sykes collected herself. "Minerva. We need your help." She spoke through gritted teeth.

Minerva laughed. Conquest's voice didn't have the quite power of War's—no one heard the screams of steel and men when she spoke. Camilla still flinched.

"Who needs my help, mortal?" Minerva demanded. She leaned forward on her desk, bracers clicking on the glossy wooden surface. "You? That weak lunatic who now rules Discord? Or are you speaking for my brother now?"

Camilla bared her teeth, eyes bright. "He certainly can't speak for himself."

Minerva stared at her for a protracted moment, enough to feel her begin to squirm. When Camilla looked away, Minerva leaned back in her chair and folded her arms across her chest.

"Say what you've come here to say, Horseman. I have quite a bit of work to do, and no time to waste on you." She twined threads of irritation and dismissal in her tones, watching Camilla carefully.

Again the mortal swallowed back a response and waited a beat before speaking. "Listen," she laid out, "when I said 'we', I meant everyone, the whole damn Family. I know you don't think of me as your sister, and I don't expect it, but Apollo's prediction—we need a plan, and Alexander says—"

Alexander says! thought Minerva, Oh my brother Ares, it's oddly good to know you're still in there.

"—you're the only one he'd trust to have a chance of being both smart and realistic." Camilla's voice was urgent. Minerva noted Camilla's fists, clenching and unclenching. The mortal woman likely wanted to pace off that nervous energy, burn it off before it exploded. Excellent.

Minerva drawled, "Really." She wondered idly how much she could push Camilla before the mortal would lose her temper.

Camilla's eyes widened as though she'd been slapped. "Yes, really, dammit!" That hadn't taken long. The young were so easy to provoke. It was a deplorable lack of control, but was doubtless pleasing to Ares' fiery nature. Minerva smoothed a frown from her brow before her brother could note it and point out her displeasure to Camilla. It would be best to keep them both guessing.

Camilla gave in to her body and began to pace, nervous energy bleeding off her. "Alexander, Ares, whatever name you want to use, he's been on me the entire night, trying to brainstorm a way to save the Family, even the ones he can barely stand." Camilla threw a hand up in the air. "You can't all expect to cheat fate the way he did."

Minerva raised her brows. "I don't believe Fate has been consulted in this matter."

Camilla let that jab bounce off. "Well, maybe someone should try!" Her dark gaze raked Minerva scornfully.

That was actually a valid suggestion. Smiling to herself, she filed it away for later.

Camilla sighed explosively, like a petulant teenager. "Listen, please. I don't know why, but Alexander cares about you—about all of you. And thanks to this whole …" She groped for words, frustration writ large on her features. "This situation, I care too." She spread her arms wide. "I don't want to care, but I do."

That tickled her. Minerva's lips curled into a reluctant smile. "Camilla, I find myself pleased to hear it."

"What? Why?" Camilla wrinkled her nose, incredulous.

Minerva leaned back in her chair, and watched Camilla relax a notch. "Because a soldier is much more effective when she cares."

Camilla grimaced. "Glad to be of service." She looked up, sharp as her sword.

"Does that mean you'll help? You'll help the Family beat this?"

Minerva blinked at her slowly. "This may not be something we can beat, Camilla." Her upraised hand cut Camilla off before she could object. "However, that doesn't mean we can't try." She bared her teeth. "And I do not like to lose."

Camilla laughed, dark and bloody as Ares' laugh ever had been. "Good for you." She raked her loose hair away from her face again to give Minerva her full attention. "So. What can I do?"

Now we start the clock, Minerva thought. "I want you to collect as many of the Family as will meet together and bring them to Lake Olympus tomorrow."

"Strategy meeting?" Camilla nodded as she turned away, thoughts already on her task.

Minerva felt a snarl twitch her lips, and gentled it into a smile. "You'll all see when you get there. I have plans already." She absently touched the diamond at her throat, smile dimming. "Tell them all that it will be well worth their time."

Camilla raised her brows at this, but grinned toothily. Minerva quashed her involuntary shiver at the horror of War's smile carved out with Camilla's lips. The girl was likely unaware as of yet how it affected others. "I'll see who and what I can motivate, Sarge. I'm guessing Hermes will help. Daybreak tomorrow?"

"Yes. And Camilla?"

"Yeah?"

"It's general, not sergeant." Conquest leaned again across her desk, this time extending one hand. "Welcome to the Family."

Somehow, Minerva managed not to gag on the words.

Dave Svenson smacked the side of his monitor hard, making it wobble precariously.

"Dammit," he hissed. His shares were down, lower then they'd been all quarter, and with a review looming, he couldn't have that.

"Quit abusing the merchandise, Dave. IT isn't going to give you any new tech until next quarter. Besides, the NASDAQ doesn't give a shit if your screen breaks."

Sarah Butler shared Dave's cube, and he hated her for it. Not that he minded sharing with a woman, not at all. He minded sharing as a concept.

Sarah took his bitter glare with typical calm. She kept her long black hair in a tight bun at the nape of her neck, a severe look that went well with her tailored suits and unadorned face. The fact that she had the face of a goddess made adornment unnecessary. Dark, heavy-lidded eyes and petal-soft lips distracted her competitors long enough for her to snap up their prize deals and use their bent backs as stepping stones.

Dave wouldn't be the next stone, though. He and Sarah had been sharing the same cube for the past six months, longer than either of them had kept a cube mate. Price insisted that her people share cubes; she said it fostered competition, and it sure as hell did. The losers moved out, the winners moved up. He knew he had to find a toehold on Sarah soon. Stalemate was almost as bad as losing.

Shrugging, Sarah turned away. Dave was about to throw her a rude gesture and get back to his numbers when his computer pinged. He glanced back and felt a jolt of excitement mixed with fear. A group IM had popped up on his screen from Price. She had sent it to a blind copy group named "Top producers".

Come to my office now.

Dave leaped to his feet, almost knocking over his chair. Sarah pushed it back as she, too, stood up. Two other heads popped up above the cubicle walls. Curt and Nala.

Sarah snorted quietly. "I guess we all know who the top producers are now."

Ignoring her, Dave locked his computer screen and took off toward Price's office, blazer in hand, determined to get there first. He spared a quick gleeful thought for Sarah's impractical heels and hobbling skirt and looked back to catch her eye. She was following him demurely, movements unhurried and smooth. Unruffled. In command.

Dammit, thought Dave. He felt heat building in his armpits, sweat misting his temples. He pushed it into his longish hair and shrugged into his blazer as he scuttled through the cubicle maze, gathering curious stares. He beat Nala by only a few feet. Fast, for such a tiny person, but not as fast as Dave.

He raised his right hand to knock, and Nala ducked under his arm and pushed the door open. Dammit! Dave forced his expression into a calmer configuration and followed her in with Curt breathing down his neck and Sarah strolling behind with a smile on her lips.

They had all been in Price's office before, but Dave still found the long, echoing walk to the desk harrowing. The coworkers bunched together instinctively and slowed to a stop before Price's command center. The old woman watched them, hands steepled against her lips, enigmatic as an owl. After a few nerve-wracking moments, Price rose to her feet and braced herself on her wide desk, arching one eyebrow when Curt sucked in a breath.

Apparently, she didn't have time to follow up Curt's stumble. Her uncanny yellow gaze swept the four of them. Dave shivered.

Price smiled, predatory. "Clear your calendars for the next few days," she announced, "I've got something more important for you four."

Nala stiffened. "My accounts—who will be handling my accounts while I'm gone?" Dave was glad someone had asked that, and extremely glad that it hadn't been him. Stumbling in front of Price was a veritable death knell.

"I will," Price said. Dave's eyes widened, and he was sure the other three looked as taken aback as he felt. Price was like Midas with stocks. If she would be managing their accounts, the commission this month would be huge.

"Go home," she told them, "and pack for a management retreat. Be here at 6 AM sharp tomorrow morning. I'm chartering a limousine for us." She reached up to touch her diamond necklace and stood up straight as an arrow. "You have an hour to set your accounts in order for me."

Curt sputtered, blinking furiously. "What do we bring? We don't even know where we're going!"

"That's part of the test, Curt. Now get moving, all of you. Tomorrow will be exciting."

Sarah nodded and immediately headed back toward the doors. The rest of them were left scrambling in her wake.

Dave cursed to himself and notched an imaginary tally mark in Sarah's column.

21208172R00083

Made in the USA
Charleston, SC
11 August 2013